sundae
my prince
will come

Also by Suzanne Nelson

Cake Pop Crush

You're Bacon Me Crazy

Macarons at Midnight

Hot Cocoa Hearts

Donut Go Breaking My Heart

Serendipity's Footsteps

sundae my prince will come

Suzanne Nelson

SCHOLASTIC INC.

Copyright © 2018 by Suzanne Nelson

All rights reserved. Published by Scholastic Inc., *Publishers since 1920.* SCHOLASTIC and associated logos are trademarks and/or registered trademarks of Scholastic Inc.

ISBN 978-1-338-19310-7

10 9 8 7 6 5 4 3 2   18 19 20 21 22

Printed in the U.S.A.   40
First printing 2018

Book design by Jennifer Rinaldi

For Isabella, Florida sunshine girl
and wonderful, beloved niece

—S.N.

Chapter One

"Okay, ladies!" Ms. Faraday called, standing in front of the studio's mirror. "*Pas de chat* now. One, two, three, and . . ."

I took a deep breath and pushed off my left foot into a leap to the side. Returning my feet to fifth position, I repeated the movement. My heart hopped along in time, already anticipating the *brisés* and *grand jetés* that would follow these smaller warm-up jumps. I enjoyed the barre work that began every ballet class, and the waltzes and pirouettes that followed as we moved to center work. The jumping, though, had always been my favorite.

"Lovely, Malie," Ms. Faraday said, and I smiled at her praise, especially since she didn't give it easily.

I focused on my reflection in the mirror. Every part of me—my black leotard, pink tights, gauzy pink skirt, and pink ballet slippers; my thick black hair pulled tightly into its sleek bun; my determined and glittering dark eyes . . . they all needed to convey *serious dancer*.

"Arresting eyes," my dad had said the day I was born. "Full of purpose." Only none of us knew what kind of purpose, until my very first ballet class. I felt it the moment I gripped the barre and did my first *plié*. Dance felt like a long-lost memory, like something that had been a part of me forever. And that was it. At age four, I was a goner.

I noticed my left wrist sagging slightly and adjusted it, wanting nothing less than perfection. From the corner of my eye, I could see Violet Olsen's jumps, which were nearly flawless. There were twenty dancers in our class, but Violet and I were the most advanced. Having her next to me made me work that much harder, and the sweat that had been pricking my temples before began to flow in earnest. My thighs and calves burned, but it was a feeling I relished, one that meant my muscles were working.

"Libby, watch your *retiré*," Ms. Faraday told one of my other classmates. "Extend your right leg. That's better."

Now it was time to finish with *fouettés*. Tchaikovsky's overture to *Swan Lake* drifted through the air, my pulse hummed, and everything fused—the music, my mind, my body—until my bends and arcs melded into fluid motion. I forgot about the bodies spinning around me, the hardness of the floor beneath my feet, the sweat trickling down my forehead. There was nothing but the exhilaration of dance, the one thing I loved more than anything in the world.

I was so absorbed that it took me a few seconds to register Ms. Faraday calling the class to a close.

"Well done, darlings." We all applauded, as we did at the end of every class. She nodded toward each of us in turn. "I have some news. First, I know you've all been waiting to hear which ballet we'll be performing this spring."

Every year, the Marina Springs Conservatory performed a ballet in the grand theater in town. Last year, it had been *Sleeping Beauty*.

"*Swan Lake*?" Libby called out from behind me.

"*Coppélia?*" Natalie asked from across the room.

"*Romeo and Juliet?*" I ventured.

Ms. Faraday shook her head, smiling. "*Cinderella!*" she announced. There were squeals around the studio. When the noise died down, Ms. Faraday added, "Auditions will be held on May first from three to eight p.m. I hope every one of you auditions."

Adrenaline flooded my veins. *Cinderella.* Maybe this year I would finally be chosen as the principal ballerina! I'd tried out for principal last year, but Violet had gotten the part; I'd been in the chorus—the *corps de ballet.* Violet was really good. Her posture was always ramrod straight, even as she walked the hallways of Marina Springs Middle School, where we both went. Her legs were long and graceful, and she kept her red hair perpetually pulled back in a knot, like she was ever ready to perform. I had to admit to her talent. It was her attitude that I'd never much liked. I could see it on her face now—the confident smirk-smile that said she knew she was a shoo-in for Cinderella. At this year's auditions, I vowed silently, I was going to give her plenty of competition.

"Now for the second announcement." Ms. Faraday pressed her palms together. "It pains me to say it, my dears, but I'm leaving you."

My heart dipped to my toes. I'd known this moment might be coming; Ms. Faraday was elderly, and there had been rumors swirling around the conservatory that she would be retiring soon. But Ms. Faraday had been my ballet teacher for the past eight years. I couldn't imagine dancing without her. Protests rose up in gasps and hushed "no's."

Ms. Faraday smiled sadly. "I've been teaching nearly half a century, and it's high time I retired." Her voice trembled only slightly. "But not to worry! The conservatory has already found a superbly qualified replacement. An email will be sent to your parents with details. And you have the audition to focus on. So I don't want anyone wasting a moment in gloom. Understood?" Reluctant nods swept the room. "All right, then. Monday will be my last class with you. We will make it our best one yet. Now." She waved her hands toward the studio door. "Shoo, shoo."

A couple of girls left, but many lingered, forming a forlorn circle around Ms. Faraday. I stayed on the outskirts of the circle, and so, I noticed, did Violet.

There'd been many times over the years when Ms. Faraday had devoted extra time to me after class, working with me on my form or a particular dance combination. She'd pushed hard, but I'd welcomed the challenge. Now I hoped to thank her in a one-on-one moment. Violet, though, stepped in front of me and threw her arms around Ms. Faraday, her eyes filling.

"It won't be the same without you!" Violet cried dramatically.

"You'll be fine, my dear." Ms. Faraday patted Violet's hand, then extended her other hand toward me, clasping my fingers with her own knotted ones. "You both will. You two have such talent, my swans. Keep sculpting it." She smiled. "And I'll be speaking to your new instructor, to advise that she put you both on pointe."

Every cell in my body shrieked with excitement. Pointe! It was the news I'd been hoping for since my twelfth birthday, when my pediatrician said my bones were strong enough for it. Going on pointe meant moving to another level of difficulty, a level where you were taken more seriously, where your dancing matured into something more complex. Now it was going to happen at last!

"Thank you, Ms. Faraday. That's amazing." I beamed.

"It is, Malie," Ms. Faraday said, smiling at me fondly.

"Mother will be so happy," Violet chimed in. "She was having a hard time understanding what was taking so long."

I stifled my urge to roll my eyes. I knew it was Violet herself, not just her mom, who was antsy about Violet going on pointe.

But if Ms. Faraday saw through Violet's ruse, she didn't point it out. Instead, she said, "Remember, you dance for yourselves first, for the love of it. Your audience comes second."

We both hugged her, and I got choked up as she pressed her hand to my cheek, whispering, "I know you'll make me proud." She turned away quickly, dabbing her eyes with a dainty handkerchief, and I knew it was time to go.

Violet and I left the studio and headed into the changing room together. It was empty now, our other classmates having left already.

"That's so sad about Ms. Faraday leaving," I said, unzipping my dance bag. I used my towel to wipe the sweat off my forehead.

"Yeah," Violet said with a shrug. "But I'm so glad the ballet is *Cinderella* this year. I've wanted to dance that part since forever. It's like Ms. Faraday chose that ballet with me in mind."

I sat down on the bench. "Or . . . maybe she chose it because it has a large cast, so there are more opportunities for everyone."

"Mm-hmm," Violet said, as if she couldn't care less about opportunities for anyone else. She slid a pair of yoga pants over her tights, then shouldered her dance bag. "We all know that the auditions for the principal are just a formality." Her practiced smile never wavered. "Don't we?"

I returned her smile, not wanting to give off as much as a hint of uncertainty. "Who knows what will happen?" I replied breezily. "Cinderella was the underdog, and look how that turned out."

"True." She laughed and headed for the door. "See you in school."

I gritted my teeth. Maybe she didn't mean to be snarky. Maybe she was just oblivious? Or . . . not.

I took off my worn ballet slippers, instantly missing the welcome hug of their elastic and leather around my feet. I frowned, examining the hole in the toe. I needed a new pair, but when I'd brought it up to Mom, she'd responded with a harried, "We'll see, *keiki*."

Even though we'd moved to Florida from Hawaii when I was a toddler, Hawaiian still peppered Mom's speech and, by default, mine. Mom said it was a way of honoring our Polynesian ancestry. Plus, she hoped it would stay fresh in my mind. After my parents' divorce three years ago, Dad had moved back to Oahu, and I visited him there each summer. Mom thought keeping up with my Hawaiian would make me feel less like a tourist when I stayed with him. She was happy to help me keep a healthy relationship with Dad. And there wasn't much that made her happy these days.

New ballet shoes, I knew, would be on the *very* bottom of Mom's list of things we needed to buy. I'd probably have to keep living with these for as long as I could. I slid them into my bag, then changed back into my street clothes. I left the dressing room, dance bag in hand, and walked through the hallway past the row of studios toward the exit.

After so many years, the conservatory felt like a second home to me. I took classes here five times a week: four weekdays after school, and once on Saturday mornings—today.

Before I left the building, I paused, setting down my dance bag. I remembered the *fouettés* I had done earlier, and was itching to try them again. Just one more time, before I had to leave and rejoin the real world. I couldn't help it; if it were up to me, I'd be dancing every second.

Even though I was in my street clothes and sneakers, I rose up on my toes, held my arms out in a circle, and began spinning. One, two, three—

Wham!

Suddenly, something smacked into me. I tumbled back to the floor, stunned.

"Pardon me!" a boy's voice said, and before I could catch my breath, strong hands were lifting me to my feet. My eyes focused on the boy before me. He had obviously just come in from outside, and he looked to be about my age. His tan skin and walnut-brown eyes were set in a square-jawed face framed by tousled black curls. "You are not hurt?" he asked.

Italian? I thought, guessing at his thick accent.

"N-no," I stammered, realizing his hands were still cupping my elbows. I stepped back.

"I am glad of this." He smiled. His teeth were slightly crooked in a cute, adds-character kind of way. "Mama would be very upset with me if I troddened on a dancer."

Troddened? "Do you mean trampled?" I asked.

"Trampled." He mulled over the word. "But this is what stampeding elephants do?" He laughed. "I'm Alonzo Benucci." So I'd been right. Italian. "Lanz for short."

"Malie Analu," I said.

"Nice to meet you, Mole-y," Lanz said.

I smiled. "Not 'mole.' It's pronounced like 'shopping mall.' Like 'Molly.'"

"Malie," he tried again, this time correctly. "So. Malie *does* smile."

My smile widened against my will. "Occasionally."

He shook his head. "That is not often enough."

I stiffened. He didn't even know me, but he was commenting on how much I smiled?

"Are you looking for someone here?" I asked. "Or are you a new dance student?"

His laugh was an exploding "Ha!" Totally uninhibited, but also magnetic. "I am picking up some paperwork for my mother. I am a gelatician. Not a dancer."

"Oh. Right." I wasn't about to let on that I didn't have a clue what a gelatician was. "That's . . . interesting."

"More delicious than interesting." His eyes twinkled, and I wondered if he saw through my charade. "But you *are* a dancer. A serious one."

I swallowed uncomfortably. "What makes you say that?"

"I saw you dancing as I walked in," he replied.

Right. My *fouettés*. This whole conversation was making me incredibly self-conscious, but I couldn't pinpoint why. I checked my watch. Oh no! How had I lost track of so much time? It was running into this boy (literally). He'd made me lose every rational thought in my brain.

"Once upon a Scoop!" I snatched up my dance bag from the floor. "I have to go! I'm late! Mom's going to kill me."

Lanz laughed. "It cannot be so bad as that?"

I didn't answer. I was already barreling through the door, then running down Main Street through the balmy late-morning heat, dreading having to face Mom.

Chapter Two

I entered Once upon a Scoop through the kitchen's back door. The hum of the giant silver machine in the middle of the room meant that Mom had started a batch of fresh ice cream. I saw containers of chocolate and coconut flavors on the counter. She must have been making Coconut Castle—one of the parlor's signature flavors.

I pulled my ruffled purple apron over my head and then checked the timer. The ice cream had five minutes left before I could empty it into five-gallon storage containers and move those to the flash freezer.

"Malie?" Mom's voice was a command, blasting from the front of the parlor.

"Coming!" I called, slipping on the fairy wings that finished off my "uniform." I walked through the swinging door into the pastel-blue room with its castle mural and white café tables.

Once upon a Scoop had a prime location on Ocean Lane, the biggest beach thoroughfare in downtown Marina Springs. The parlor offered a sprawling view of the pale sand and azure waves of the Gulf Coast. Dotted with mangroves and palms, the beach, about thirty steps from the parlor's front door, brought in a steady stream of customers. Some lived in Marina Springs full-time, relishing its warmth and sun. Others were what we Floridians called "snowbirds," visitors who came south for a few months each year to escape harsh northeast winters.

With the boutiques and outdoor restaurants, and the pink bougainvillea lining the sidewalks, our small town was a perfect vacation spot. The view from the shop's window was one of the things I liked about working at Once upon a Scoop, but today I only had a millisecond to take it in before Mom blocked it with her stern gaze.

"You're fifteen minutes late." Her voice was granite.

"I didn't mean to be. Ms. Faraday made a big announcement—"

"Malie, you always have an excuse. I'm not in the mood today." Mom turned and hurried behind the counter. "Help me put these flavors in the freezer before we open."

"Okay," I said, following her. I'd tell her about Ms. Faraday's big news later.

Mom handed me a tub of Snow White, its white-chocolate ice cream dotted with chunks of cheesecake and yogurt-covered pretzels. I dutifully placed the tub into the display freezer.

"When you started taking the advanced dance classes at the conservatory," Mom said, handing me another tub, "it was under the condition that it wouldn't interfere with your schoolwork or with Once upon a Scoop, but now... I thought you'd outgrow this dance phase."

I frowned. "It's not a phase. It's what I love." I'd said it before. *So* many times. My talks with Mom lately were like a glitch in a song—we started out fresh at the beginning, but inevitably hit a faulty chord and skipped back to the same spot, over and over again. It always came down to dance.

Mom sighed. "Your responsibilities here come first."

"I don't get it," I persisted. "When Dad was here, you never complained about my ballet. You *wanted* me to take lessons!"

The worry lines on Mom's forehead deepened. "Some things were simpler then."

Like money, I thought. The Marina Springs Conservatory was considered the best ballet school in west-central Florida. It had an aura about it—an atmosphere of gravity and respect that emanated from the very floor and walls. When I'd auditioned in kindergarten and been accepted, I'd been beyond thrilled. Ever since then, I'd imagined going all the way, joining a professional ballet company someday. But I didn't understand back then what a stretch it was for my parents to pay the conservatory's tuition. And since the divorce, it had only gotten tougher.

"I never thought you'd stick with ballet this long. And when your dad was here, he could help out at the parlor. Now I'm—" Mom stopped before adding, *by myself*. She was thinking it, though. I'd overheard her talking on the phone with Tutu, my grandma in Oahu. It was the only time Mom had admitted that being a single parent was tough. She never said it to me.

"I want her to grow up without having to worry about me," she'd said to Tutu. "Lots of people raise children on their own, with less than what we have. If they can do it, I can, too."

I worried, though, especially whenever Mom got the look she wore now—the carrying-the-weight-of-the-world-on-her-shoulders look. That look swept the wind right out of my arguing sails. It made me pull her into a hug and give her a peck on the cheek.

"It will be okay, Mom. I won't be late again."

"I'm being a grouch today," Mom said. "I'm sorry. It's Mr. Sneeves. He isn't happy with us."

I snorted. "Is he *ever* happy?" Mr. Sneeves was the parlor's owner, a stuffy micromanager who constantly criticized the way Mom ran the parlor. I couldn't stand him.

"Respect, *keiki*!" Mom scolded. "He stopped by earlier to remind me about the spring break crowd. He wants the parlor open for extended hours. We'll have to triple our ice cream stock."

I squeezed her hand. "We can handle it. You're the ice cream queen!"

When we'd moved here, the idea of my mom managing an ice cream parlor seemed like a dream come true. I had visions of sundaes for breakfast, lunch, and dinner. But working at the parlor was not easy. And once I fell in love with ballet, things like schoolwork, chores, and especially Once upon a Scoop—they all conspired to keep me from dancing as much as I wanted. So even though it was still *kind* of fun to come to an ice cream parlor every day, a lot of the appeal was lost.

A knock sounded on the parlor's front door, and I turned around. My best friend, Tilisha, stood outside with her boyfriend, Andres. Behind them, scribbling in a notebook, stood my boyfriend (it still felt funny to think that word), Ethan.

"Help! Let us in!" Tilly was hollering.

"Before it's too late!" Andres cried. "Before he infects us!"

I laughed. Mom rolled her eyes and waved at me to let my wacky friends inside.

My friends were regulars at Once upon a Scoop. On weekdays they stopped by after school, between extracurriculars.

Saturdays, though, were special. They showed up at 11:30 a.m. like clockwork, for what Tilly had dubbed their "VIP access." This meant they got first dibs on the fresh ice cream before the parlor opened at noon. Then they'd hang out for a while, playing Heads Up! on their phones while I helped my mom. I might not love the parlor like I did when I was little, but I loved that my friends had adopted it as a regular meeting spot.

I unlocked the door, and Tilly and Andres burst through it. Tilly hugged me, her dark brown braids tickling my cheek.

"*Please* rein in your boy, Mal," she told me, nodding toward Ethan. "He's been zombified. Next he'll harvest our brains in the name of science."

"Only if you keep trying to toss my invention log into the ocean." Ethan walked into the parlor, shaking sand from the pages of his notebook. His sea-green eyes caught mine, and his serious expression morphed into a smile. "Hey, you."

"Hey yourself," I said, reaching for his hand.

It had been six months since Tilly had officially deemed Ethan and me a "couple." Ethan and I had been friends since kindergarten, forming a tight foursome with Tilly and Andres.

When Tilly and Andres started dating over the summer, it seemed expected that Ethan and I would accompany them on their movie dates. One day, while Tilly and Andres were holding hands, Ethan took my hand, too. It just felt like the natural next step. And then, in front of my locker at school, Ethan gave me my first-ever kiss—a quick peck on the lips. And that was that. Tilly pronounced us boyfriend and girlfriend, and the four of us settled into an easy routine.

Mom had always insisted that boyfriends should be reserved for high school, or even college. But since Mom had known Ethan and his family forever, and since Ethan and I always hung out in a group, she'd warmed up to the idea.

Now, holding hands with Ethan felt as familiar to me as a *plié*. I barely thought about it anymore, except to appreciate the cozy comfort of his palm resting against mine.

"Yes!" Andres shouted, making a beeline to the display freezer. "Goldichocs and the Butterfinger Bears. My fave!" Andres loved to eat, but you wouldn't know it from how beanpole-skinny he was. He opened the tub and tried to dip a finger straight inside, but Mom caught his hand.

"Andres! Where are your manners?" she demanded.

"Please, Makuahine," Andres said. "One bite? I have baseball practice this afternoon. I need stamina!" *Makuahine* was my friends' pet name for Mom. It meant *mother* in Hawaiian, and calling her that, Andres knew, was the way to her heart.

Mom shook her head, but she grabbed a cup and scooped him up a hefty helping. She didn't mind dishing ice cream for my friends, but she always made a show of being strict about it first.

Tilly gazed out the window. One of the town's landscapers was pruning a palm tree on the other side of Ocean Lane. "Why are they tossing those fronds in the Dumpster?" she asked, horrified. "They can repurpose those as mulch!"

I shrugged, but Tilly was already out the door. No wonder my best friend was the president of the Environmental Conservation Club at school. I watched as she chatted with the surprised landscaper and I wondered if "101 Uses for Palm Fronds" would be the next feature in her popular *It's Easy Being Green* blog.

While Tilly worked her recycling magic and Mom finished

scooping Andres's ice cream, Ethan and I sat down at our table by the window. I recognized the look of intense concentration on his face. He got it whenever he worked on a tough problem, which, considering that he took advanced science courses at school, was pretty much all the time.

"What's wrong?" I asked.

"I'm stuck on the wiring for the surfboard propeller," he said. "It has to be waterproof but also equipped with sensors to detect signs of distress." Ethan had an idea for a lifesaving surfboard that could pull a surfer to shore safely. "But if I use rubber instead of plastic . . ." He was gone, whispering to himself and scribbling notes in his log.

I looked at Andres and Tilly (who'd just returned, grinning victoriously). They shook their heads in unison.

"He gets like this every spring," Andres said forlornly. "And we become obsolete."

"Poor baby," Tilly told him. "Suffering from a bromance broken heart."

I giggled. "Don't worry. The school's Invention Convention will be over next month, and then you'll have him back."

Andres and Ethan had been best buds since kindergarten, and Andres took it personally when Ethan's inventing sprees disrupted their hang time. I, on the other hand, never minded. I was driven in dance; Ethan was driven in science. Whenever Ethan backed out from movie dates or school dances at the last minute, I told him it was fine. He did the same for me when I canceled on him to squeeze in extra dance practice.

Tilly put her arm around Andres. "No pouting today. You're *way* cuter without the frown."

Andres's expression softened. He never could stay grumpy around Tilly.

"So, who's in for Heads Up?" Tilly asked, pulling out her phone. "I'm guessing Science Guy is out. What about you, Mal?"

"You have to play," Andres said to me. "How else am I going to crush your winning streak?"

"*That's* not happening." I stuck out my tongue at him, then shot a glance at Mom, who was logging today's ice cream stock on the parlor's iPad. "I don't know . . ." I leaned toward them. "Mom's been riding me for showing up late today."

"I heard that!" Mom piped up. "Okay, okay, you can have some fun, Malie. But only until the shop opens."

I nodded, grateful. While Ethan scribbled in his notebook, the rest of us played two rounds, laughing hysterically when Andres tried to act out the word *modeling* by strutting through the parlor wearing Tilly's wedge sandals. That one even got a chuckle from Ethan, but he refocused on his work seconds later.

Before I knew it, Mom was tapping me on the shoulder and gesturing toward the front door, where a line of customers was already forming. It was noon. Time to open.

I stood reluctantly. "I'm out. Scoop detail."

"Okay," Tilly said. "We'll hang here for a bit . . ."

". . . and try not to distract you," Andres put in.

Ethan raised his head long enough to smile at me and say, "Good luck with the crowds."

"Thanks." I opened the door, letting a swarm of guests in.

By the time I took the twelfth order, I saw Ethan stand up, disgruntled by the noise. He grabbed his notebook and gave me a call-you-later hand signal.

I nodded and blew him a quick kiss. Tilly and Andres stayed for a while longer, but even they got tired of the crowd and headed for the beach. In the meantime, I kept scooping. And scooping . . . and scooping. At some point, my mind drifted away from ice cream. I pictured an empty stage with a single, gleaming spotlight. Then I was in that spotlight, spinning pirouette after pirouette. The crowd in the parlor transformed into an audience, holding its collective breath, waiting to see how many turns I could make. My entire body was poised, exhilarated. And then . . .

"Malie! The scoop!" Mom nudged my shoulder. I blinked, looked down, and saw my scoop poised in midair, dripping ice cream all over the floor.

So much for applause. I adjusted my crooked fairy wings, then leaned over another tub of ice cream. Where was *my* fairy godmother when I needed her?

Chapter Three

"Malie?"

I could make out my mom's voice over the classical music sweeping through my earbuds.

I blinked. Oh . . . right. It was Monday morning. I was *supposed* to be getting ready for school, but instead I was standing in my bedroom, using my dresser as a barre, and . . .

"Choreographing in your head again?" Mom looked even more tired than usual. When I'd gone to bed last night, she'd still been at the kitchen table of our small apartment, paying bills and sighing over every one. Never a good sign.

"I can't help it," I said, taking out my earbuds and putting my phone down. It was impossible for me to hear the music and not envision the moves that might accompany each trill of a violin or cello. When I glanced down at my feet, they were in third position. I was ready to dance even in pajamas.

Mom sat down on my bed, taking in the posters of Misty Copeland hanging on my walls. Misty was my idol—a ballet goddess who'd defied every rule by advancing faster in her dance career than anyone ever thought possible.

"It's quite a collection you have here," Mom said. "I never noticed . . ." She mumbled these words to herself, as if she was realizing something for the first time. She pinched the bridge of her nose—something she did right before sharing bad news. She'd done it when she and Dad announced their divorce, and again when they'd told me he was moving back to Hawaii. I felt suddenly nervous.

"Malie," she began, "I got an email last night from the conservatory, telling parents about the new dance instructor."

"Great!" I sat down beside her. This wasn't bad news at all. "Who is it?"

"They've hired someone from overseas. French, or maybe Italian, I can't remember." She fidgeted with the bedspread, avoiding my eyes. "Apparently, she's famous and was in high demand. And now . . ." She took a deep breath. ". . . the conservatory's raising tuition costs to help pay her salary."

My throat constricted. "By how much?"

"They're doubling it." The resignation in Mom's voice was like a death knell. "And—I hoped I wouldn't have to tell you this—but the rent's going up on our apartment, too. I found out last week. With the higher rent and now the tuition . . . we can't afford the conservatory, *keiki.*"

My dread rushed headlong into panic. "What? Well, maybe I can cut back on my classes. Go only twice a week. Or . . ." My mind scrambled for possibilities. "What about scholarships? I can apply for one—"

"I already asked about that. Ms. Faraday and I have been emailing back and forth since last night. She'd love to help, but the conservatory doesn't offer scholarships, *or* abbreviated schedules." Her mouth was a grim line. "I'm afraid you'll have to quit."

The world buckled. I pressed my fists into my roiling stomach. "But . . ." *No dance?* I couldn't even say it out loud. It was too unfathomable. "No!" I shut my eyes. "This can't happen now! I'm going to audition for *Cinderella*. I'm ready for pointe, and—"

"I'm so sorry, Malie, but not anymore."

I felt a wave of nausea. I could just imagine Violet gloating when she found out I was dropping dance. Without me auditioning for the part, she'd be a sure bet for the lead in *Cinderella*. I believed—*really* believed—that I'd had a shot, too. How could I give up this chance? My lip trembled.

Mom watched me worriedly. "Malie, this is my fault. After everything that happened with the divorce, I wanted you to keep some stability. Dance was what you loved, so I allowed it to continue." She grew quieter. "I knew the day would come when you'd have to start thinking about more realistic goals, when you'd have to realize that dance is a hobby, not something you devote your life to."

I stared at her, not believing what I was hearing. "Dance is *not* my hobby. It's so much more than that."

Mom frowned. "It's a distraction for you, and it takes up too much of your time." She clasped her hands in her lap tightly. "It's better for this to happen now, before you advance any further. We can't pay for you to keep studying. There's a limit to how far you would've been able to go—"

"You don't know what I might be able to do!" My voice rose an octave.

"It doesn't matter. I need more of your help at the parlor anyway. There's nothing to be done about it."

Tears brimmed in my eyes, but I stood up quickly and walked over to my closet. I didn't want to argue with Mom. So much of this wasn't even her fault. If I stayed in this room a second more, I'd unleash every ounce of my anger and sadness at her. I threw on clothes, pulled my hair into a messy side braid, and grabbed my schoolbag.

"I have to go." I hated the telltale quiver of my voice.

Mom looked stricken. "You need breakfast—"

"Not hungry." I hurried from the room, Mom's voice calling after me, then fading into the distance as I burst out of our second-floor apartment and down the flight of outdoor stairs that led to the street.

I ran the two blocks to school, rushing past the tourists with their boogie boards and beach totes, who were scanning the ominous clouds overhead. A rumble of thunder sounded, and blue lightning streaked the sky. Storms often blew into our town from the Gulf, barreling over us in a fury and leaving everything clean, fresh, and new. This morning, the dark clouds mirrored the storm inside me.

Go ahead, I challenged the sky when thunder cracked again, louder this time. *Bring it on.*

The first raindrops fell like hard pellets, stinging my cheeks, and camouflaging the tears that fell with them.

• • • • • • •

I dragged myself into Marina Springs Middle School, drenched and miserable. I didn't bother wringing out my waterlogged hair and streaming clothes. It felt fitting that puddles should form wherever I stepped in the school's hallways. It was like my own personal river of mourning.

I caught sight of Ethan up ahead, his back turned to me. His blond hair was cutely disheveled and the Invention Convention notebook under his arm was overflowing with wrinkled pieces of paper.

I blurted his name when I was still a few feet away, my frustration pouring out. "You're not going to believe what happened. The conservatory doubled its tuition, and Mom says—"

"Whoa, whoa, slow down." He turned to face me, his eyes widening. "You're drenched! What's wrong?"

Every thought I'd had on the tip of my tongue faltered. Because, I realized, Ethan wasn't alone. He'd been standing facing a boy with tan skin and curly dark hair. It was the boy I'd run into at the studio on Saturday. The Italian boy.

The boy was looking at me now with the same mischievous grin, his eyes glinting like he'd just finished laughing at some hilarious joke. The memory of our collision hit me, and my heart gave an unsteady thump.

"Lanz, right?" I asked, knowing that my tone sounded rude but too upset to care. Why did he have to be here right now, in a moment when I so desperately needed to talk to Ethan?

"That's right. And you're Malie like 'shopping mall.'" He

cocked his head, and a lock of his black hair slid forward. His grin widened as my face reddened. Ethan looked back and forth between the two of us in confusion.

"You've met already?" Ethan asked.

"For a second," I said quickly.

"A painful second," Lanz said. "She pirouetted across my foot."

I frowned, bristling. "Hey, I didn't—"

He broke into laughter. "I made a joke. That's all."

"Oh. Okay." I fumbled with my braid, something I did when I was nervous. Only . . . *why* was I nervous? I wasn't. I was annoyed. Or maybe nervous *and* annoyed.

"Lanz was at the conservatory this weekend," I explained.

Ethan nodded, as if that made perfect sense, which baffled me even more. "Lanz just moved here from Verona, Italy," Ethan told me. "He was in the office getting registered when I dropped off my Invention Convention permission slip. Principal Thorton asked if I would give him a quick tour of the school before the bell rang."

"I do not need a tour." Lanz pushed a hand through his curls.

"In new places, I like to find my way with . . . how do you say, 'happy accidents'?"

"It wouldn't be a happy accident if we were tardy," I said, checking the hall clock. The bell was about to ring and I hadn't even talked to Ethan about the dance disaster yet. Now there wasn't a chance of it happening until later. "Our hallway monitor, Ms. Cad, gives out detentions like candy." At Lanz's blank look, I explained, "A detention is when you have to stay after school as punishment for being late to class."

"Ah, yes, I have gotten those before." He smiled, like detention was a pleasant thing. "Sometimes on purpose."

"Why would you do that?" Ethan looked shocked.

"I nap best in detention," Lanz explained. "And if I stay after school, I have less time for chores at home. Brilliant, yes?"

Ethan laughed. "I never thought of that. Maybe I'll give it a try."

Not a chance, I thought. Ethan didn't have a rebellious bone in his body, especially when he had to maintain an A average to participate in the Invention Convention.

"Come on, Lanz," Ethan added. "I can show you where the caf is on the way to class."

"Wait," I said to Ethan. "I need to talk—"

"Right." Ethan slapped his forehead. "I forgot. You started to tell me something? What happened?"

I hesitated. I didn't want to pour my heart out in front of Lanz. The idea of it made me feel too . . . exposed, like he'd be drawing his own conclusions about who I was the whole time. Or worse, what if he laughed? That seemed like something he might do.

The bell rang. "Never mind." My spirits went from bad to abysmal.

Ethan squeezed my hand. "See you later?"

I nodded, but when Lanz glanced down at my hand in Ethan's, I felt another wave of self-consciousness. What was up with me? I held hands with Ethan at school every day. Why should I do anything different just because someone new was taking notice?

"*Ciao*, Malie," Lanz said. There was that grin again.

I stiffened. He was so confident. *Too* confident.

I watched them move down the hallway, Ethan with his pur-
poseful, I-have-places-to-be walk, Lanz with a crooked saunter.
What if they became friends? As I walked to class, I found myself
hoping that they wouldn't. I couldn't quite explain why, but I
didn't want to see too much of Lanz.

● ● ● ● ● ● ● ●

Three hours later, I saw from my spot in the lunch line that Lanz
had made himself at home already. I knew Ethan was eating
lunch in the science lab, as he always did in the weeks leading up
to the Invention Convention. But Lanz hadn't had any trouble
finding people to sit with. Tables full of kids waved him over.
And Lanz didn't choose just one table, the way most kids did. He
moved between tables, greeting everyone with his carefree smile.
He seemed just as comfortable talking with the soccer team
as he was with the chess club, and gauging from the laughter
erupting from each table, everyone found him über-entertaining.
I tried not to stare, but it was hard not to.

When he glanced up at one point, our eyes locked, and I
instantly looked away.

"What a poseur," I whispered to Tilly, who was studying the

sloppy joe on her tray with suspicion. She transferred the sandwich to Andres's tray, adding to the two there already.

"Who? Lanz?" She hummed a low note, a sign that she was about to call me out on something. "Doesn't that seem a wee bit harsh? He's only been here for a half a second."

I frowned in Lanz's direction. "Nobody makes friends that fast!"

We paid for our lunches and walked out into the dining area. Tilly set down her lunch tray at our table with a definitive clang. "Mal, you're having an epically bad day. And I don't blame you for being totally peeved."

I nodded, happy for the validation. From the second I'd told Tilly about the ballet news in homeroom, she'd been brainstorming ways for me to keep dancing. Granted, some of her ideas were over the top (i.e., running away to New York City and camping outside the American Ballet Theatre in hopes of meeting Misty Copeland to ask for her help). But I loved her for refusing to accept reality without scouring for every possible solution. Unlike Ethan. When I'd finally managed to tell him about it in between classes, he'd been sympathetic but also matter-of-fact.

"Try to see it from your mom's point of view," Ethan had said. "She's doing the best she can." I knew that was true. But I wanted him to take *my* side instead of taking his "reason over emotion" approach. I wanted someone telling me how unfair it was. Tilly was doing exactly that, and then some.

Only right now, when I thought she was going to let me get away with my dig at Lanz, she said, "I know you've got ballet angst, but that doesn't give you a free pass on snarkiness."

I sank onto the lunch bench, groaning. "You're right. It's just . . . there's something about him that . . ." That made my neck prickle? That made me simultaneously want to stare at him and avoid seeing him ever again? "He's . . . too much."

"I think he's legit," Andres said between bites of sloppy joe. "His locker's two down from mine, and he has this Italian chocolate. Perugina? He was giving pieces to everybody in the hallway, just to be nice."

Tilly smacked Andres's shoulder playfully. "You think everyone who gives you free food is nice."

"Hey! It has to be *good* food." Andres laughed as Tilly and I rolled our eyes. "I'm only saying that, even with the ballet stuff, you shouldn't blame the guy for who his mom is."

"What?" I looked at Andres blankly. "What's his mom got to do with anything?"

Andres glanced from me to Tilly. "Oh man. You haven't heard. Soooooo, Lanz's mom is the new instructor at the Marina Springs Conservatory of Dance."

I dropped my head to the table. "Of *course* she is!" Mom had said the new teacher was from overseas. I looked up at my friends in disbelief. "So *she's* the reason the tuition doubled!"

"She must be an amazing teacher," Andres said, then yelped when Tilly elbowed him.

"*Not* helpful," she hissed, and he shrugged apologetically.

I stood up with my lunch tray. "I'm not hungry anymore. I'm going to hang in the library until the bell."

Tilly put out a hand to stop me. "Tell me you're not going to torture yourself by watching Misty Copeland YouTubes." When I didn't answer, she sighed, then stood. "I'm coming."

"You don't have to."

She hugged me. "No wallowing alone. It's our besties rule."

"Don't argue," Andres advised me. "You know how she gets when she's on a mission."

That was true. I remembered the time Tilly got it in her head that we should take a class trip to the Everglades to learn about conservation; she hadn't backed down until our teacher agreed to it. Then there was the time she convinced Andres, Ethan, and me to adopt a sea turtle nesting site. Tilly was intensely loyal to all her causes, which also made her a great friend.

Feeling grateful, I linked my arm through hers and we headed to the library together.

I could only hope that the rest of this day wouldn't be as bad as the beginning.

Chapter Four

Later that afternoon, the storm had passed. As I walked from ballet school to Once upon a Scoop, the weather was sunny and fresh, with a salty breeze wafting from the ocean. Downtown Marina Springs bustled with people shopping and eating at the outdoor cafés. The vacation-y atmosphere only darkened my mood. I'd just had my very last class with Ms. Faraday, which had been hard and emotional. I knew it was likely my very last ballet class—ever.

When I turned the corner and spotted a line of customers outside the parlor, my mood only got stormier. Now I was going to have to put on a happy face for dozens of strangers.

And—even worse—there was Lanz, standing in line. My heart fluttered and heat rose to my face.

"Malie! How lucky to see you!" Lanz said, stepping out of line and walking over to me.

"Lanz." My voice was wound tight. "What are you doing here?"

"What is everyone else doing here? It is hot today, so . . . ice cream, of course!" When I didn't return his smile, he added, "Our apartment is not far from here, so I went exploring and found this . . ." He tilted his head back to read the sign over the door. "Once upon a Scoop."

The name of our parlor sounded charming in his accent, but I refused to even crack a smile. "It looks like you're going to have a long wait," I told him. "And you got out of line."

He shrugged. "This doesn't matter. I have time." He took a step toward the end of the line, motioning for me to follow. "It will go fast with company."

"Oh no," I blurted. "I'm not here to buy ice cream. I work here. My mom's the manager."

To my surprise, Lanz's eyes lit up. "This is even better than I hoped," he said with obvious delight.

"I'm, um, not sure what you mean?" I shifted my schoolbag, and he reached to slide it from my shoulder.

"Please, let me take it." His fingers brushed my collarbone, and a shiver ran through me.

"No. Really," I sputtered. "I'm fine." But the bag was already off my shoulder, my protests ignored. "So, um . . ." I struggled to find my train of thought. "Why is my working here such a good thing?"

"Ice cream! I have, um—how do you say in English—skill with the ice cream?"

"Eating it?" The sarcasm in my voice was obvious, and I silently scolded myself. I had no reason to be treating him this way. But everything about his cheery, outspoken manner seemed to rub me the wrong way.

He laughed, looking disarmingly cute. "Eating it, of course. But also making it. I told you before. I am a gelatician."

"Um, what *is* that?" I asked.

"Ah. This word is maybe not familiar in English? My father owns a gelateria in Verona," Lanz explained. "He taught me how to make gelato. Ice cream, also." He motioned to the line outside the parlor. "You're very busy. And maybe I can help."

"You want to work *here*?" My stomach sank further when he nodded, his eyes hopeful. "We're not hiring." My voice was clipped. "The parlor's on a tight budget." That was true. Mr. Sneeves wouldn't let Mom hire any more employees. He said without more sales, he couldn't spare the expense.

"Budget?" Lanz repeated, and I could see him silently translating that into Italian in his head. "Oh no!" he exclaimed. "I don't need pay. I would enjoy helping. I have many ideas for flavors, and—"

"The parlor owner won't let someone volunteer to help out. There's paperwork, and . . . and . . ." Now I was making things up as I went along. Yes, Mr. Sneeves had a lot of rules. But I was technically an unpaid volunteer, and Mr. Sneeves had never said anything to Mom about *me* not being allowed to work at the parlor. "You can't work here. I'm sorry."

Lanz stared at me. For the first time, the smile was gone from his face, replaced by bewilderment.

"No, I'm the one who's sorry. I am causing you upset." He handed me back my schoolbag cautiously, almost shyly. The poor guy had just moved here from across the ocean, and here I was, being the *unwelcome* wagon. "I only thought that you might need someone to fill in for you sometimes? Maybe while you're at your dance classes?"

I flinched, feeling an almost physical pain. "I—I can't take ballet anymore."

He caught the quiver in my voice and took a step toward me, his eyes intent on mine. "But why? This was why you looked so sad this morning at school. Yes?" His expression was so focused, like he already understood me. How was that even possible? He was just trying to pull his charm act on me. I was *not* going to fall for it.

"Just . . . never mind. The reason's not important."

"You forget. I've seen you dance." His voice softened. "I think this is not your decision, but someone else's. Made for you. I think that you would never give up dance on your own. You love it too much."

What was he doing, dissecting my soul? "The tuition at the

conservatory just got doubled, okay?" I snapped. "It's too expensive now, and it's all because of, because of . . ." *Your mom*, I wanted to shout, but stopped myself as I saw understanding dawn on his face.

"Oh, I see," he said quietly. "I am sorry." He paused, thinking, and then his face brightened. "But . . . what if there was a way we could help each other?"

"I don't see how."

"My mother is the new director at the conservatory."

"I heard." There was no disguising the terseness in my voice. "She must be a great dancer."

He nodded. "When she married my dad, she was a principal dancer at the Teatro alla Scala in Milan. She danced with the company for ten years before she had me."

Wow. That *was* impressive. I hated to admit it, but it made sense that the conservatory was doubling the tuition, with an instructor of that caliber coming on board.

"My mother searches for new talents," Lanz continued. "If she sees you dance, perhaps she may take you as a private student."

I shook my head. "I already told you. The tuition—"

Lanz waved his hand. "This is where my idea comes for helping each other. You can let me help you at Once upon a Scoop, because ice cream is what I love. And in return, my mother teaches you."

"But . . . we couldn't pay you. And I can't pay her."

"I only want to make ice cream. And my mother, she wants me to have a tutor. To help me with my English. So . . ." He snapped his fingers. "I will practice English with you and work at this parlor, for free. You will practice dance with my mom, for free. *Capisce?*"

It seemed too much to take in at first, too impossibly lucky that this chance should fall into my lap. My heart thrilled. The world, which had seemed darker this morning, brightened again. I could keep dancing, and maybe even talk to Lanz's mom about *Cinderella*, to see if I could still audition. Possibilities pirouetted before my eyes.

Then just as quickly, my hopes fizzled. I couldn't work with Lanz. If I did, well . . . I'd have to be near that charming smile, and those curls, for hours at a time. Suddenly, a vision of Ethan appeared before me, his eyes full of purpose and scientific calculations.

No, I told myself. Working with Lanz was *not* a good idea. It was a *very* bad one. But . . . if it gave me a chance to dance again? How could I possibly say no?

"I . . . I don't know. I'd have to think about it, and check with my mom. But . . . not today. Things here are too hectic." I'd put it off as long as possible, I decided.

Lanz opened his mouth, probably to argue, but he never got the words out, because a demanding "Malie!" boomed from the parlor.

Uh-oh. Mom. She was standing in the doorway.

"Inside now," she said.

"I have to go," I mumbled to Lanz. But instead of walking away, Lanz followed me to the door.

"Signora Analu?" Lanz smiled at Mom. "I'm so sorry I kept Malie from her work. Please. It's my fault. Not hers."

"Well." Mom huffed, wiping her brow. "She should've kept an eye on the time. And the line. We're swamped. And you're out here chatting away with . . . with—"

"Lanz Benucci." He shook her hand. "A friend of Malie's from school."

I could only answer Mom's questioning look with a shrug.

"Since it's my fault Malie is late," Lanz went on, "I'd be happy to help in the parlor. I think . . ." He nodded toward the line. ". . . you need it?"

Mom shook her head, and I felt a wave of relief. She wasn't going to let him stay. "Mr. Sneeves won't like anyone who's not an official employee working with the ice cream. It probably violates health codes, or liability, or—"

"Excuse me," a red-faced customer interrupted, "we've been waiting for over fifteen minutes . . ."

A chorus of rumbling agreements rose from the line.

"We'll be right with you!" Mom called, looking increasingly desperate. Then she added to us, "I don't have the time to deal with this." She headed for the sales counter and called over her shoulder, "Just . . . come in and let's see how it goes. *Please* don't break anything."

Lanz grinned triumphantly. "Looks like you are stuck on me," he said.

"It's stuck *with* you," I corrected him. "Come on. Let's get to work."

• • • • • • •

"Don't touch that!" I said as Lanz reached for the buttons on the silver ice cream machine. "It's, um, fragile."

"Really?" Lanz's eyebrows rose in surprise. "It doesn't seem so very different from the ones we use in Italy."

"The buttons are moody," I explained.

"Ah." He nodded.

We'd been in the kitchen for about five minutes, which was already five minutes too long. Usually, I felt chilly in the kitchen, because the AC was blasting while I handled cold ingredients. Today, though, my skin was flushed, and my heart hadn't stopped hammering. As Lanz moved around the kitchen, studying our machinery and supplies, I noticed everything about him, from the way he grazed his fingers along the countertops to the way his curls sloped across his right eyebrow. I *would* put a stop to the dizzying effect he had on me.

"And . . . this is your deep freeze unit?" He moved toward the freezer.

"Don't worry about that," I said. "You won't be using it."

He turned to the ingredients lined up in the containers on the counter, and his eyes narrowed.

"You use these . . . *caramelle gommose* in your ice cream?" he asked doubtfully.

"Gummy bears." I nodded.

"And . . . this *gomma da masticare*, too?"

"Bubble gum. Sure. Little kids gobble it up. It's the neon colors, I guess."

His eyes widened, and if I hadn't been so intent on staying annoyed with him, I might've laughed at his expression. It wasn't an expression of distaste, or haughtiness. It was an expression of legit horror.

"But where are the fresh ingredients?" he asked. "Fruit from the market?"

"We use canned fruit."

"What about pastries?"

I shook my head. "We use store-bought cookies and candy."

He clutched his chest, falling back against the counter, then shook his head so violently his curls bounced across his forehead. "Never! My father uses only fresh ingredients."

I rolled my eyes. "This isn't your dad's ice cream shop." For a second, sadness flickered over his features. I felt a pang of guilt, guessing I'd hit on a sore spot. I could've asked him about it, but decided not to. I didn't want to get to know him too well. "Besides," I added, "you're not going to need to work with any of the ingredients."

He leaned against the counter, folding his arms and giving me that playful, taunting smile. "Okay. Tell me, what *am* I allowed to do? Count the gummy bears? Or maybe watch ice cream freeze?" So he *had* noticed my cold shoulder. I blushed and opened my mouth, but before I could respond, he laughed. "You're trying so very hard to get me to dislike you. I hate to disappoint you," he added with a grin, "but it's not working." My face burned hotter. "I'm not giving up, but I *am* going to help your mother. I'm pretty sure she'll agree that I'm safe with a scooper."

He stepped through the swinging doors, leaving me in

stunned silence. The instant he was gone, the kitchen took on an empty, bland feeling. *Great*. I'd gotten exactly what I'd wanted, and now I wished I hadn't.

For the next half hour, I tried to keep busy, starting a new batch of Goldichocs and restocking all of the jars of dried toppings.

When I went out front, I noticed the change in the atmosphere. The customers who'd been grousing about the long wait were now laughing and chatting happily. Lanz was scooping ice cream like a pro, as if he'd done it a thousand times before, and Mom looked so relieved that even she seemed cheery. Lanz was joking with the customers, charming them even as he explained that we'd run out of their favorite flavor.

"Why not try something fresh and new?" he coaxed one little girl. "A Mad Hatter Mango to match that blonde hair?" With another he teased, "Watch out for Pinocchio's Pistachio. It will make your nose sprout like a tree!"

It seemed impossible for anyone to dislike him. Except, possibly, me.

Finally, there was nothing left for me to do but grab an ice cream scoop and join Mom and Lanz behind the counter.

"The rush is dying down," I said to Mom as I drizzled hot fudge over the banana split order she'd just handed me.

"Finally." Mom rang up the banana split for one of the last customers. "Thank goodness Lanz works so quickly."

He held up his scoop. "And no customers were injured in the scooping of this ice cream."

Mom laughed, and my heart sank. Great. Lanz had charmed Mom, too.

As Mom began wiping off a few of the tables, Lanz stepped to my side.

"So. *Now* do you approve?" he asked.

"Of what?" I dropped my eyes.

"Of me working here?"

"He impressed me so much today," Mom chimed in, "that I told Lanz he's welcome to help anytime."

"You don't need *my* approval." I tried to turn away, but his gaze stopped me.

"But I do," he said quietly, so only I could hear. His expression grew thoughtful. "I'm not sure what I've done to make it so, but I feel that you find me . . . unbearable?"

"No—"

"*Per favore*." He held up a hand. "It is simple. If you don't want me here, I won't come."

I *didn't* want him here, but what choice did I have? If I didn't agree, I'd lose my chance at dancing.

I shrugged, pretending that it made no difference to me one way or the other. "Work here. Whatever. It's fine by me."

"*Molto bene!* And tomorrow, I will bring all fresh ingredients. And we will make new ice cream. So delicious! You'll see."

I nodded, then made my escape into the kitchen. What was I getting myself into? *Dance,* I reminded myself. *I'm doing this for dance.* Dance was everything. And Lanz? I would get used to having Lanz around, and soon I'd forget that he'd ever had this strange, intoxicating effect on me.

Chapter Five

"Let me get this straight." Tilly leaned against her locker, twisting one of her braids around her finger. "You still have a shot at dancing, *and* you have someone to help your mom out at Once upon a Scoop. And you're *unhappy*?" She raised one eyebrow doubtfully.

"You make it sound ridiculous." I stifled a yawn. I'd barely slept last night, my mind whirring over the predicament I found myself in. "And I'm *not* unhappy. It's just . . . the whole working with Lanz thing."

"What's wrong with Mr. Congeniality?" She smoothed out her KEEP CALM AND LET AN ENVIRONMENTALIST HANDLE IT tee.

I balked. "You don't even know him. What if it's a disaster?"

"Why would it be?" She gave me a quizzical look.

"I—I'm not sure we'll get along," I said helplessly.

"He's befriended the entire student body in under two days. Plus, he seems to be taking his new job seriously."

"Yeah right." I scoffed, thinking of how little he seemed to take anything seriously.

"Well. Andres and I ran into him on Main Street last night. He was looking for the Marina Springs Ice Cream Shop. Checking out the competition, he said." She paused to let this sink in. The Marina Springs Ice Cream Shop was Once upon a Scoop's biggest competitor. Last year, the shop had beaten us for the town-voted honor of "Best Ice Cream in Marina Springs." Mr. Sneeves had been grouchier than usual after we lost the title. "So maybe he really *is* as good at ice cream as he says he is," Tilly said. When I could only shrug, she added, "What does Ethan say about it?"

My irritation burbled fresh. "Not much of anything." I'd called Ethan last night, hoping I'd feel better after talking with him. But he'd been distant and distracted. All I'd heard were monotone "uh-huhs" and "mmms" from the other end of the line.

"Ethan?" I'd blurted. "Are you even listening?"

"Oh sure!" he'd said quickly. "Of course I am!" I'd heard clanging and rattling in the background.

"You are not! You're working on your invention." Normally, I would've laughed it off. It was one of the things I'd found cute about him—the absentmindedness combined with intense focus. Last night, though, I'd found it annoying.

He'd sighed. "You're right. I'm sorry, but I think I finally had a breakthrough on the sensors in the wiring. If I don't work on it now, I might forget—"

I'd swallowed, a stab of hurt streaking through me. Ethan was a sweet guy. Logic said I should remember that, but it was tough to be logical when I felt so out of sorts. Shouldn't a girlfriend in distress trump schoolwork? "It's okay," I forced myself to say. "Go back to your work."

"Thanks. We can talk tomorrow?"

"Sure," I'd said. Then I'd tried to ignore my frustration, without success.

Now, I took some of it out on my locker, slamming it shut while Tilly's eyes widened.

"Hold up. You're mad at Ethan, too?" Tilly asked. "You two *never* fight."

"We're not fighting," I said glumly. "Only, I needed him to listen last night, and he was . . . well, he was Ethan."

"No surprise there." Tilly snorted. "You wouldn't be going out with him if he weren't Ethan."

I gave a small smile. "That's true."

"Malie! There you are." Lanz's voice called from behind me, and I turned to see him breezing down the hallway in cargo shorts and a rumpled white shirt. His hair was disheveled, like he'd rolled out of bed mere moments before, and he was eating a chocolate croissant. I wanted to look away but couldn't.

"You must come to the conservatory after school," Lanz said, stopping in front of me. "I talked to Mama, and she's agreed to watch you dance."

My heart leapt. "Really? Wow. I . . . didn't expect you to ask so fast."

"Of course. I didn't want you to miss any more dance than

you had to. And . . . I worried that you'd change your mind about me working at the parlor." He winked. "I know it pains you."

"Wha—no, it doesn't!" I lied as Tilly's shoulders shook with silent laughter.

"Don't worry about Mal, Lanz." Tilly patted his shoulder. "It's just that she doesn't enjoy anything about ice cream anymore. Maybe you can change her mind."

The bell rang then.

"So I will meet you at the conservatory after school?" Lanz asked.

"I'll have to grab my ballet stuff from home first, but I'll be there," I replied, my pulse a drum in my ears. Forget my confusion over Lanz. This was my shot, and I wasn't about to blow it.

• • • • • • •

"Are you ready?" Lanz asked as we stood outside the conservatory.

I swallowed. "To meet your mom, who used to dance with Teatro alla Scala, one of the best dance companies in the world? Sure. Why not?" I choked out a laugh. "It's not the least bit intimidating."

The sidewalk was bustling with sunburned tourists. They all seemed so relaxed and happy, completely oblivious to the fact that my entire future was dependent on the next few minutes. (Or at least, that's what it felt like.) I had my dance bag in a stranglehold, and I couldn't seem to make my feet take another step.

"Don't worry," Lanz said earnestly. He put his hand on the door, then paused. "Only . . . if you are terrible, you may want to duck."

"Duck? Why?"

"To avoid getting hit in the head with a pointe shoe." He shrugged. "She throws them sometimes, but only in disgust."

I felt my face pale, but then I caught the glint of amusement in his eyes. "No, no. I'm not falling for it this time." I shook a finger at him. "You're joking, right?" I was finally starting to figure him out.

He didn't answer, but only held the door open for me, bowing slightly as he did. "After you."

"You *have* to be joking," I said as we stepped inside. We

walked from the hallway into the familiar studio, with its long mirror and wooden barre.

"Miss Analu." The silken but imperious voice belonged to a black-haired woman whose facial features resembled Lanz's in everything but her smile. Whereas Lanz's smile was so easily given and casual, Signora Benucci's was like her movements, poised and exacting. She stood in front of the mirror, her hair piled on top of her head in a bun. She held a single pointe shoe in her right hand, which she tapped against the palm of her left. Was it for throwing? My heart tripled its pace. "We have only a few minutes before the afternoon classes begin," she continued in her thick Italian accent. Her English was perfect. "Time is of the essence."

"Yes! I'll be quick." I hurriedly slipped my yoga pants off and slid into my ballet shoes. I glanced at Lanz, who nodded toward the pointe shoe in his mother's hand, then grinned.

"I'll wait outside, yes?" Lanz said.

He'd asked me, but his mother was the one who answered with a clipped "*Sì*," followed by a string of more Italian that I couldn't make any sense of, but sounded like it might've been a scolding. *Oh no*, I thought. *Maybe she's already decided I'm a waste of her time.*

If that was the case, Lanz showed no sign of it. He just nodded good-naturedly and gave me a thumbs-up before leaving.

"My son tells me you can dance." Signora Benucci touched her phone's screen, and the familiar overture to *Swan Lake* flowed from the room's speakers. She swept her arm out as way of invitation. "Show me."

For a second, every shred of confidence left me. Then, as the music swelled, my body quieted my mind, and I began to dance. This was the part I loved—when my limbs acted on their own, moving as an extension of the music. My spine seemed to stretch and lengthen as I moved from fourth position into a series of pirouettes, then segued into an *arabesque*.

I forgot Signora Benucci was watching. I forgot where I was. *When* I was. The music consumed me, and I molded to its form.

"Thank you, Miss Analu!" The loudness of Signora Benucci's voice meant that this was the second, or maybe even third, time she'd tried to get my attention.

"Sorry," I blurted, sweeping my right foot in an arc across the floor. My nervousness returned full force. "I get lost in the dancing sometimes."

"It *should* consume you." She gave a single, knowing nod. "As George Balanchine once said, 'I don't want people who want to dance, I want people who *have* to dance.'" She tapped the pointe shoe against her palm. "Tell me, Miss Analu. Which type of person do you believe you are?"

"I don't believe," I responded without a second's hesitation. "I know. I *have* to dance. And I will." I sucked in a breath, then continued, "I was planning on auditioning for *Cinderella*. I don't know if that's still possible, but . . . that's not all. I want to dance in a company someday and—"

"Those are big dreams, Miss Analu. There will always be others more advanced than you. *Better* than you."

I nodded. "I want to dance at *my* best. Misty Copeland didn't start ballet until she was thirteen, and she was dancing professionally two years later. It *can* happen."

Signora Benucci's eyes penetrated mine, as if she were the

human equivalent of a lie detector. "And if I don't take you on as a private student? What will you do then?"

"Find another way."

She gazed at me for a few more seconds.

"Yes. I will teach you," she said, and relief swept over me. "Your technique is coarser than I would like, but you have promising form, and you move with a *passione* I don't see often. And if you progress, I will see what I can do about the *Cinderella* audition." She lifted a finger of warning. "That is not a promise. Only a chance. You will be here every Tuesday, Wednesday, and Thursday afternoon when school ends. Three p.m.?"

My heart soared. "Yes!" I gushed. "I will. Thank you so much, Signora Benucci! You won't be sorry!"

Her lips lifted in an elegant smile. "Thank *you* for helping Lanz with his English."

"What?" I said blankly, nearly forgetting about the promise I'd made to Lanz. I caught my mistake just in time, rushing on with, "Oh! Right! Yes, no problem. I'm happy to help."

She glanced at the watch on her slender wrist. "My other students are arriving shortly. So . . . tomorrow at three?"

"I'll be here," I said as I quickly changed from my ballet slippers to my street shoes. I left the studio, my entire body bursting with joy.

Lanz met me outside the dance school. Before he could say a word, I threw my arms around him, gushing, "She's going to help me! *Chee-hu!*"

It took about two seconds for me to realize I was hugging Lanz Benucci in the middle of Main Street. His arms tightened around me, and his laughter in my hair made the skin on the back of my neck tingle. Warmth flooded my body before embarrassment made me pull away, blushing like mad.

"Sorry. I didn't mean to do that."

"I don't mind. You should smile like that more often. Happiness brings out the amber in your eyes."

"What amber?" I scoffed. "My eyes are brown."

Lanz shook his head. "They have an amber rim. Like a halo. It's *bellissima*. Beautiful."

My heart fluttered, and I dropped my gaze, tongue-tied. No one had ever noticed that about my eyes before. Not me. Not Ethan. Ethan . . .

"I have to text Ethan!" I cried. "And Tilly! They wanted to know how it went." I pulled out my phone to text them, but then when I saw the time, I groaned. "I didn't realize how late it is. I've got to get over to Once upon a Scoop."

"I'll come, too," Lanz said. "Last night, I made a list of recipes. And—" He picked up a small cooler that had been sitting by the door. "I have some special ingredients." He gestured to the windows high above the conservatory. "I grabbed them from our apartment while you were dancing for my mother."

I didn't have time to ask Lanz what was in the cooler, or to try to dissuade him from coming. I was too grateful to him, and too stressed about the time. I nodded, and off we ran toward the ice cream parlor.

Chapter Six

Lanz and I stepped inside the kitchen of Once upon a Scoop to find the counters strewn with spilled sprinkles, toffee crumbles, and chocolate chips. And Mom in the middle of it all.

"Malie, where have you been?" Mom hissed, her eyes flashing. "Mr. Sneeves is here."

She pushed open the door toward the eating area a crack, and I could see Mr. Sneeves's familiar bald head and gray suit as he went from table to table, asking customers how the ice cream was and if the service was satisfactory.

"Five minutes after he showed up, I accidentally knocked over a bunch of containers." Mom brushed a stray hair from her forehead. "I haven't had a chance to clean them up yet because the line's been nonstop. People are complaining to Mr. Sneeves about the long waits. *And* the soft-serve machine has been acting up."

"I'm sorry, Mom. I know I'm late, but you'll understand when I tell you what happened." I nearly laughed with excitement. I'd wanted to tell her about Lanz's idea last night, but the second we'd gotten back to our apartment, she'd started paying bills and her mood went steadily downhill from there. Her mood didn't seem much better right now, but maybe she'd be relieved that I'd found a solution to the dance problem that wouldn't cost us anything. "See," I pushed on, "I stopped at the conservatory and—"

"What?" Mom frowned. "You knew I expected you right after school and you wasted your time there doing . . . what? Saying hi to your dance friends?"

"Mrs. Analu." Lanz stepped to my side. "I can explain—"

"Thank you, Lanz, but I don't need you to make excuses for Malie." She sighed. "What I *need* is for my daughter to accept her responsibilities. Not force them on her friends."

Mom walked through the door into the front area, and I followed her, not believing what I'd just heard.

"That's so unfair!" My voice was rising, and several customers looked up from their sundaes. "I've never—"

Mr. Sneeves cleared his throat. "Mrs. Analu, please," he told Mom, his tone quiet but stern. "Whatever family drama this is, the customers do not need to be a party to it."

"I'm sorry, Mr. Sneeves. It won't happen again." Mom turned to me. "Malie, can you please prepare a vanilla soft-serve cone for the next customer?"

I marched over to the soft-serve machine, trembling with pent-up anger. Mom hadn't even given me the chance to explain!

When I depressed the soft-serve handle, a whine rose up from the machine's depths. I ignored it, only wanting to be done with this order as quickly as possible. Suddenly, smoke began pouring from the back of the machine. Its whining rose to a shriek.

"Mom!" I cried, and she flew to my side, unplugging the soft-serve machine and fanning away the smoke. A collective groan rose up from the customers.

"Don't worry, folks." Mr. Sneeves's voice rose silky smooth over the complaining. His mouth was smiling, but his eyes certainly weren't. "This is just a small malfunction. We'll have it fixed in no time. And in the interim, I'm happy to offer two free scoops for everyone."

Some people nodded, while others kept grumbling.

Mr. Sneeves examined the soft-serve machine, his jaw flexing. "This machine is past its service date," he said quietly to Mom. "No wonder it overheated. I'd like a word outside?"

Mom paled, and guilt gnawed at me, dulling some of my anger. "It's okay," I told her. "I can handle things here. It'll be fine."

But the moment Mom and Mr. Sneeves stepped outside, customers began grumbling all over again.

"Please," I started, "I appreciate your patience—"

"We're out of patience!" one teenage boy piped up from the back of the line.

"But wait!" a familiar accented voice called out. "You haven't tasted *this* ice cream yet." It was Lanz, who'd appeared from inside the kitchen, holding a tub in his arms. "Who wants to try our new flavor? Fairy-Tale Ambrosia."

"What are you doing?" I whisper-hissed. "We don't have that flavor."

He set the tub on the counter. "We do now. I made it last night at home." He gave me an imploring look. "Trust me. For a little while? *Va bene?* Okay?"

I hesitated, then looked at the crowd of frowning faces before me. At this point, I didn't have a choice. I nodded.

Lanz grinned, popped the lid off the tub, and slid it into an empty slot in the display. "Who would like the first scoop?"

• • • • • • •

An hour later, the parlor was empty, and so was the tub of Fairy-Tale Ambrosia. I peered at its scraped-clean bottom, bewildered.

"I don't know what you put in that ice cream, but it worked like magic," I said. "I've never seen people's moods change so fast." The customers had gone from grouchy to beaming almost the instant the Ambrosia touched their lips.

"It's the crushed *formiche*," Lanz said with a smile. Together, we headed into the kitchen to start a new batch of ice cream for the next day. "Works every time."

"Four-me-kay?" I mangled the word. "Is that a special Italian ingredient?"

"In English, I believe the word is . . . 'ants'?"

I glanced warily at his cooler, which now rested on the kitchen counter. "You mean, the six-legged crawling kind of ants?"

"Of course! What other kind would there be?"

"Oh. My. God." I sank against the counter, covering my mouth. Eeeeeww. I seriously hoped there weren't any more creepy-crawly ingredients in that cooler right now. How was I going to explain *that* to Mom? She'd returned from her talk with Mr. Sneeves looking even more stressed, and since the afternoon rush finished, she'd been in the back office crunching numbers. "I'm . . . not sure how Mom's going to feel about bugs as an ingredient."

He burst out laughing. "I am making a joke! There were no ants in the ice cream. Only macaroons and marshmallows."

"Oh . . ." I shook my head, flustered. "Joking . . . right."

He tilted his head at me. "This joking. You don't do it very often?"

"No," I mumbled. "Ever, actually."

"Well," he said quietly, peering into my eyes. "Maybe you should try it. Your mom, I think, needs laughter."

My stomach clenched with sadness. I thought I was the only one who noticed. "Mom didn't used to be that way," I said softly. "She used to laugh all the time." I smiled, remembering. "She'd sing in the shower. Led Zeppelin and Bon Jovi. Loud enough that we could hear her from the other side of our house. She's completely tone deaf, but Dad and I promised each other we'd never tell her."

"So . . . what happened?"

"The divorce." My voice tightened. "Mom and Dad split three years ago, and since then Mom's stressed all the time."

"My parents divorced, too." Lanz began lifting Tupperware containers from the cooler. "A few months ago. That is why we moved to Florida. My aunt lives in Fort Myers, not far from here. Mama wanted to be closer to her and to our cousins. She thought the change would be good for us."

I nodded. "I'm sorry. Divorce stinks."

"*Marcio*. Rotten." Lanz nodded. "I am glad that they do not fight anymore. My parents. Only . . . I miss us together, too, even with the fighting."

"I totally get that. It's hard on my dad not being able to see me, and it's hard on my mom being by herself. She's lonely, even though she doesn't want to tell me she is."

"Yes. My mother also," Lanz said quietly. "She is angry, too. My papa and I . . . we both love creating new flavors, experimenting with food. It is something we shared. Mama didn't understand this, or how much time my dad spent at his gelateria. And now . . ." He sighed. "She doesn't even like me talking about it." His carefree expression dimmed. "I made the Fairy-Tale Ambrosia last night with the ice cream maker Papa sent me as a moving present. We used to make ice cream together, but . . . no longer. He wanted me to have it since he can't be here with me."

"You miss him." It was written on his face, even through the upbeat tone he was striving to keep. "And that doesn't seem right of your mom. I mean, she knows you love your dad."

"She does. Maybe just the hurt is too . . . fresh for her? The ice cream maker my papa gave me? She says it's *una spina nel fianco*. In English, I think you say, a prick in her rib?"

"A thorn in her side," I corrected him gently.

He laughed. "Yes . . . that. English is still confusion at times."

"Confusing," I said, then giggled despite myself.

Lanz looked at me in surprise. "So you do laugh after all!"

"I do . . . when something is actually funny."

He clutched his chest. "Now I am wounded."

"I doubt that." I gave him a sideways glance. "It doesn't seem like much bothers you."

He shrugged. "It bothers me the way my mother speaks of my father. They couldn't get along? *Così sia*. So be it. Only I wish for all of us to be in *amicizia*. Friendship?"

"That's one thing about my parents' divorce that went okay," I said. "They still talk to each other, mostly about me. It's not like it used to be, but it's friendly enough. I just wish Mom were happier."

"I think sometimes my mother looks at me and sees my father. She seems unhappy then, and I feel bad for causing her unhappiness." Lanz hesitated. "I have a confession." It was the first time I'd ever seen him looking sheepish. "I haven't told Mama that I am working here. Only that you are helping me with English. I . . . didn't want to disappoint her."

I absorbed this as he waited for my reaction. "I haven't told my mom yet about taking lessons with your mom at the conservatory." I lowered my voice, glancing toward Mom's half-closed office door. "I was about to earlier, but then she got so angry. If I told her, and she said I couldn't keep dancing, I couldn't deal."

"What will you do?"

"I don't know yet." I swallowed down my burgeoning anxiety. "What if your mom finds out you're working at an ice cream parlor?"

"I do not need to tell her *where* my English lessons are taking place." He shrugged. "It's not lying. Only not giving details. Sometimes, it is better to jump from the nest before the mother bird sees. What can she do once you are flying?"

I laughed, and he looked proud. "Another laugh. That is two today!" Lanz cleared his throat and ducked his head. "It is strange. I have not talked about the divorce with anyone before."

I nodded. "I don't talk about it much, either. Except to Tilly. I tried talking to Ethan about it once, but—" I shrugged. "He didn't really get it."

"But he must get you," Lanz said matter-of-factly. "He's your boyfriend."

My throat hitched. "Oh, he does! Only ... he takes things literally sometimes. He says my mom can't have changed that much. That science shows it's nearly impossible for certain personality traits to change ..." I remembered how unsatisfied I'd felt with Ethan's response, as if, by not understanding what had happened with Mom, he wasn't understanding part of who I was, either. I didn't like to admit to myself that it still bugged me.

Lanz shook his head. "I'm not sure there is a science for broken hearts. Or for falling in love."

We stood in silence for a minute, letting the air around us soak up those words.

"Maybe our moms should hang out," I said, half joking. "It could help? Like a divorcée club or something?"

He smiled. "Maybe. But ... we should probably make the ice cream first?"

I laughed. We'd been so busy talking, I'd nearly forgotten about it. How had that happened?

Lanz turned and opened his cooler. He pulled out a small jar of espresso beans, and then a larger Tupperware container, which contained layers of creamy custard and ladyfingers.

"What's that?" I asked.

He grabbed a spoon from the counter, dipping it into the container. "Tiramisu. It's my papa's recipe. Here. Try."

I took the spoon from him. The custard, cocoa powder, and ladyfingers made for a smooth *and* crunchy texture. The custard was rich with vanilla undertones, topped with the perfect blend of bittersweet chocolate. "Wow. This is delish."

Lanz blushed. *He looks cute wearing bashful*, I observed, then quickly brushed the thought away.

"*Grazie.* I made it last night for a new flavor of ice cream. Tiramisu, with a dash of espresso, and perhaps a homemade cookie butter swirl?" He pulled a final jar from the cooler, this one full of a caramelly spread that I could only assume was cookie butter.

"Isn't that sort of sophisticated?" I asked.

"Well, it's something fresh and new. But it can still have a fairy-tale name."

I paused, thinking. "How about Tiara-misu?" We grinned at each other in agreement. "Okay. Let's try it."

I grabbed the milk, cream, and vanilla flavoring from our fridge, then opened the top of the ice cream maker to reveal its yawning insides. I popped the lid off the milk and lifted it, ready to pour it into the machine.

Lanz stared. "But . . . what is it you're doing?"

"Making ice cream," I explained. "All you have to do is dump the ingredients into the machine. It pretty much does all the rest."

"Dump?" He repeated the word distastefully. He inspected the bottle of vanilla flavoring. "And what is this? Artificial vanilla?"

"Hey. It gets the job done."

He dropped his head. "Tragic." But even as he said it, his eyes glinted. "Ice cream needs finesse. Coaxing." He searched in the cabinets until he unearthed some large pans that I guessed hadn't seen the light of day in years. "First, we scald the milk," he said, "then add eggs. But *accuratamente*. Carefully, so they don't curdle. Eggs make the ice cream thicker, creamier. Better."

He heated the milk over the stove and then beat the eggs in a bowl, his wrist moving with an artistic rhythm. When tiny, foamy bubbles formed around the edge of the pan, he smiled in approval. "Now we add the eggs. You try."

I took the bowl from him, then poured the eggs into the pan. I gasped as globs of curdled egg rose to the surface of the liquid. "Um . . . oops?"

Lanz mock-glared. "You dumped."

I sputtered. "I did not!" When he kept glaring, I broke into giggles. "I dumped."

He took the bowl away from me. "You should stick with dancing."

I rolled my eyes. "Tell me something I *don't* know."

"Ah ah ah. I'm not letting you give up so easily. We try again, yes?" He tossed the curdled eggs down the drain, mixed fresh ones, and then handed me the bowl. I hesitated.

"Slowly and gently." He stood behind me. "Like you were performing an *adagio*." My breath caught at his use of the dance expression. As soon as he described it, I knew exactly what he wanted. He slipped his hand over mine, and I lost my breath entirely. "Like this."

Together, we trickled the egg mixture into the pan, slowly and carefully. This time, they didn't curdle.

"This takes a long time," I murmured, torn between wanting his hand to stay on mine and feeling like I should move away.

"Great ice cream is like great dancing. It takes patience and hard work. And also . . ." He flicked a bit of cold milk at me with his spoon. "Fun."

I splashed some milk back at him with a laugh. "Not everything is about fun."

"Work should bring you joy," he went on. "My father says that life is like gelato—flavorful, delightful, surprising. But always gone too soon. So . . . I try to live *la dolce vita*." His eyes studied me. "And for you. Dance makes life sweeter?"

"It does," I said. "But I'll probably never have the patience for ice cream that I do for dance. That's one of the reasons why Mom gets frustrated with me."

"Maybe search for the sweetness in the process?"

That turned out to be easier than I thought. Drawn out as the process was, the warmth of Lanz's palm against the back of my hand as he guided me made every second better. Then, guilt stung me. What if I was being disloyal to Ethan? On the other hand, Lanz and I were only making ice cream together. What was wrong with that?

Still, I tried to put a safe distance between us as we waited for the egg-and-milk mixture to cool enough to put it into the ice cream machine. I focused on washing up the pots and cleaning the counters. But after we'd poured the mixture into the ice cream machine to start it churning, adding in a splash of the espresso for flavor, Lanz pulled an edition of *The Scarlet Letter* from his backpack and sat down next to me.

"We have fifteen minutes before it is done churning," he said. "Maybe we have our English lesson now?"

"I wasn't sure you actually wanted a tutoring lesson," I said.

"Of course I do," he said, his eyes playful. "I didn't lie to my mother. I told her half of the truth? And it's not so much the speaking of English I need help with, but the reading of it.

Maybe I should read out loud, and you can help me with the difficult words?"

I nodded, we bent our heads over the text, and soon I was lost again. Not in the words, but in the nearness of him. It was confusing—completely freaking me out. What did it mean? I was terrified what the answer to that question might be.

Just then, the back door opened, and the strange spell was broken. I startled, pulling away from Lanz, and glanced up to see Ethan in the doorway, with Tilly and Andres right behind him.

"Hey—"I began, but that was all I managed to get out before the three of them rushed at me, practically knocking me over with their group hug.

"You did it!" Tilly hollered. "Congrats!"

My mind was still muddled, so it took me a few seconds to remember the text I'd sent them on the walk here, telling them about what had happened with Signora Benucci.

"Thanks, guys," I stammered.

Ethan put his arm around my waist, kissing my cheek. I was

hyperconscious of Lanz watching us together, and of Tilly watching *Lanz* watching *us*. I could practically hear Tilly's internal radar pinging. What was she seeing right now?

The ice cream machine beeped, signaling that the churning was finished. Phew! Thankful to have an excuse, I slid away from Ethan and out from under Lanz's and Tilly's gazes. I removed the metal bucket from the machine. Peaks of cappuccino-colored ice cream filled the bucket, the consistency of soft serve. It would only grow firmer after being in the deep freeze for a day.

"Time to add the tiramisu," Lanz said, "quickly before the ice cream starts to melt."

I held the Tupperware container as Lanz scooped bits of the tiramisu into the bucket. Then he added the cookie butter. He stirred only just enough to fold the dessert and cookie butter into the ice cream.

As Lanz worked, Ethan smiled at me proudly. "It's awesome news, Mal. What did your mom say?"

"About what?" Mom asked.

I whirled around to see her standing in her office doorway.

"Oh, well . . ." I hesitated. Now was my chance to tell her, but one look at her harried face warned me against it. I couldn't risk her saying no. "Just that Tilly and I have this big English project coming up," I blurted. "A Google Drive presentation on *The Scarlet Letter*." That was true, at least. "And," I continued, "we're going to need to work on it after school for the next few weeks. At Tilly's house. We have to log in our work time on Google Drive." That part? Not exactly true.

Ethan was shooting me a questioning look, wondering what I was doing. When Tilly met my gaze, I gave her a silent plea: *Back me up on this.*

"Huge project." Tilly groaned, taking my cue. "It counts for a lot of our grade."

Thank you, my eyes told her.

"Oh." Mom's forehead creased. "Well, I can't say no to a school project. But the afternoon is our biggest rush. I can't manage on my own—"

"I'll help," Lanz jumped in, shooting me a smile that made my heart dance. "I can work every day after school."

Mom thought it over, then finally nodded. "All right. But"—
she held up a finger and looked at me—"you come to the parlor
as soon as you're finished at Tilly's. Understood?"

I nodded, afraid to look her in the eyes. I hated having to lie,
but what choice did I have? I *would* tell her the truth, when
things settled down at the parlor.

Chapter Seven

"So you're lying to your mom," Ethan said as he walked me home under the hazy, moonlit sky. His voice was matter-of-fact, but there was a new, critical edge to it that made me squirm.

"I didn't lie to her about the English project." I gazed up at the moths circling the streetlamp above the sidewalk. "I just didn't tell her about the dancing. But I will."

"I can't see how this is going to work. She's going to find out."

"She is, because I'm *going* to tell her. Eventually." I stared at him. "Look . . . why are you being weird about this? I thought you'd be excited for me."

"I am!" His step quickened and his hand tensed in mine. "Was this Lanz's idea?"

"What? No!" I was glad my blush was disguised in the evening shadows. "Why would you say that?"

Suddenly, I was wishing we'd said yes when Tilly'd invited us back to her house for TV and pizza. Andres and Lanz had gone with her, but when Ethan had said he had Invention Convention work to do tonight, I'd said I was tired. Really, I'd been wary of hanging out with Lanz without Ethan, dreading that heady confusion he caused in me. What I hadn't expected was for Ethan to grill me within a minute of leaving the parlor.

Ethan shrugged. "No reason. Only . . . he's so lax with everything. And you were pretty much with him all day."

"I didn't have a choice. He had to introduce me to his mom, and he's working at the parlor now."

Ethan frowned. "You know half the girls at school have a thing for him."

"What?" There was something about his tone that gave me pause. Wait a sec . . . was he jealous?

He shrugged, giving me a small, sheepish smile. "Just saying."

"Lucky for you, Italian accents aren't my thing." I said it teasingly, but when he didn't laugh, I stopped to face him, squeezing his hand in mine. "Hey. *You're* my boyfriend, remember? And I make my *own* decisions. You know that."

Ethan nodded as we climbed the stairs to the apartment. "It's just not like you to keep stuff from your mom. I mean, since the divorce you've been . . . protective of her."

My heart squeezed in my chest. He knew me so well. "But that's part of why I'm waiting to tell her. She was in such a bad mood at the parlor today, and you know how she's been about dance." I dug my key from my pocket. "I want to find the right time, and a way to say it so that there's no chance we'll end up fighting about it."

Ethan smiled at me. "You're right. You can handle your mom. And . . . well, it's great of Lanz to have set this whole dance thing up for you."

I put my arms around him, giving him a hug. "Thanks," I said into his shoulder.

He kissed me lightly, sweetly, but as he did, my mind whirred with a new, startling question. Was this lukewarm coziness how a kiss was supposed to feel? In a flash, I thought of how my pulse spiked whenever I was around Lanz. I pushed the thought away as a shiver of guilt ran through me.

"Chilly?" Ethan asked.

"I . . . must be." I stepped inside. "See you tomorrow at school."

I shut the door, leaning against it and trying to clear my head. Yup. Chilly . . . in eighty-degree weather. That had to be the problem.

• • • • • • •

When Mom walked through the door half an hour later, I held up the tray of sandwiches I'd just finished making.

"Dinner," I announced.

"Lifesaver." Mom kissed me on the cheek and sank onto the couch. "What a day."

I set the tray on the coffee table and handed Mom her sandwich—toasted bread layered with apricot cream cheese, pineapple, egg, and ham. It was one of our long-time favorites, a

Hawaiian specialty, and easy enough for me to make without Mom's help.

The sandwich was usually an automatic mood-booster for Mom, but not tonight. As I finished my sandwich, Mom was still nibbling at hers, wearing a distant, preoccupied expression.

"Mom?" I nudged her. "Want to watch some *Gilmore Girls*?" She loved that show, but she only shook her head.

"Malie, we need to talk," she said, her voice drained. "Mr. Sneeves doesn't think I'm doing a good job managing the shop. Our menu needs updating. We need to draw in more customers, make our flavors more exotic. If I can't do that..." Her voice faltered.

"What?" I scooted closer to Mom. I hadn't seen her this upset since I was younger, back when she and Dad fought all the time.

"If I can't do that, he's going to look for a new parlor manager," she whispered.

Fury blazed a trail from my head to my toes. "He can't do that!"

"He can do whatever he wants."

"He's such a jerk." I stood up and stomped to the sink with my plate, resisting the urge to slam it onto the counter. "You've been telling him for weeks that the soft-serve machine wasn't acting right. What happened today was because he ignored you. He's—"

"My supervisor." Mom walked up behind me, frowning. "It's only because of him that I have this job."

Her voice was stern and disappointed all at once. I hated the idea of Mom answering to a boss as stony and exacting as Mr. Sneeves.

She bit her lip. "Malie, it won't just mean losing a job. I'm not sure we could afford to stay in Marina Springs—"

"Stop," I interrupted, feeling the urge to clamp my hands over my ears like a child. "That won't happen. We're not going to let it happen." A hard resolve stole over me. "There's no way Mr. Sneeves is going to fire you. We'll figure it out. We'll come up with some new flavors, and—" An idea blossomed in my head. "We'll start using all fresh ingredients. Like Lanz suggested."

She gave me a tired smile. "We'll see what happens. This isn't your problem to worry about. Only . . ." She sighed. "You were so upset over losing dance, I thought maybe if you understood more of what was going on, it might make it easier for you."

Guilt trampled my heart. "It's okay, Mom. I'm not giving up on the idea of dancing," I added cautiously. "I know I'll have more chances."

Mom put her nearly untouched sandwich in the fridge. "Your dad used to talk like that about his art. No matter how many galleries turned down his paintings, he was convinced he could still paint as a career. It would've been easier for him—for . . . us—if he'd just accepted it and moved on."

"Dad could never not paint. He'd be miserable." Dad had always been the dreamer, while Mom was the practical one. Maybe that was why Dad understood my love of dance so well. Since Dad moved back to Oahu, he spent most days on the beach painting landscapes and then selling them at a sidewalk stall to tourists. He loved what he did, but making a living doing it was another matter entirely. That had been one of the many things he and Mom had fought about before the divorce.

"Well. He made choices." Regret filled her voice. "And . . . that's that." She rubbed her temples, as if this conversation was giving her a headache. "I'm going to bed." She gave me a quick hug. "Thanks for making dinner."

I nodded, washed the dishes, and headed into my bedroom. My brain was too tangled with thoughts for sleep, so I sat in front of my laptop and FaceTimed with Dad. Seeing his smiling face always made me feel better. And since Hawaii was six hours behind us, it was still early there.

Dad answered right away, beaming. We spent a few minutes chatting easily about school and his painting. Then his expression changed.

"Kiddo," he said soberly, "your mom told me about what happened with the tuition at the conservatory." His face was pinched on the screen. "I'm sorry. I wish I could help out. I would if there was any way—"

"I know, Dad," I said quickly, wanting to get off the topic. The less I said about dance, the better.

Dad grinned. "Hey, tomorrow I could sell ten paintings and then . . ." He raised his hand in the shaka sign. "Golden."

"Golden." My voice emitted a confidence I didn't feel. As

Mom once said, Dad was the master of hanging hopes on rainbows.

"Everything else copacetic?" he asked.

I hesitated, thinking about Mom's job. It was on the tip of my tongue to tell him, but . . . no. Mom wouldn't want me to get into all that with Dad.

"Yup." My voice rose cheerily. "Copacetic!"

"Great. Oof, it's getting late, kiddo. Got to set up my booth. Love you."

"You too, Dad." I blew him a kiss and then the screen went dark.

As I got ready for bed, I wondered: Would Mom ever understand my dancing, when she couldn't understand Dad's art?

• • • • • • •

"Your *allongé*! No no no. Not like that." Signora Benucci clucked her tongue.

A line of sweat trickled down my temple. My leotard was soaked. But I didn't dare move a single muscle, or the *arabesque* I was holding would break. Signora Benucci stood in front of me, her expression strict but still kind. In the first two days of training with Signora Benucci, I'd learned that she was demanding, pushing me to the limits of my strength and endurance. She'd have me repeat a *piqué* or a *glissade jeté* over and over again until she was satisfied with my form.

"You must extend your arm, and reach," she said now. "Imagine something at your fingertips. Something you must have. Chocolate, diamonds, your heart's desire—"

I closed my eyes, holding the position, and I reached, seeing in my mind's eye what I longed for. *Cinderella*. Every muscle in my body elongated, my rib cage opened, my lungs expanded, my chin lifted . . .

"Yes! Yes!" Signora Benucci smiled. "*Brillante!* Now, move into your pirouettes. Travel. And again, again, again . . ."

I led with my chin, fixing my eyes on the corner of the studio, turning and turning, channeling flumes of energy. When I reached the wall, I stopped, breathless.

"An improvement indeed." Signora Benucci nodded her approval as she handed me a towel. "But there is still much work to do."

I caught my breath as I wiped the dampness from my neck and face. "Just tell me what I need to do, and I'll do it."

She paused, studying my face. "I believe you will."

I checked the wall clock. "I have to get going."

"Before you leave, I have something for you." She disappeared into the storage closet at the back of the studio, and a moment later, returned holding a pair of pale pink pointe shoes. "Here you are." Signora Benucci smiled as she handed them to me.

My heart leapt as I took the shoes, cradling them in my arms. I giggled in spite of myself.

"What is it?" she asked.

"Nothing. Only . . . well, for a second I thought you might throw them at me. Lanz told me—"

"That I throw shoes when I'm unhappy with my dancers?" Signora Benucci rolled her eyes. "That boy. Always the joker." She winked at me. "Although I have been known to throw a pair or two at him, when he sleeps through his alarm." She nodded toward the shoes. "I believe they're your size. Try them to see how they feel."

I took off my old ballet slippers and slid my feet into the pointe shoes. Then I slowly rose up entirely onto my toes. Suddenly, I felt taller, more graceful, as if the pointe shoes were transforming me. "They feel strange . . . but amazing."

"There will be pain," she warned. "Expect blisters and calluses. Only, for you, I think it will hardly matter. I do believe you'd dance on hot coals if that was your only option." She wagged a finger at me. "Make sure you use your arch stretcher and keep up with your exercises. Break in the toe box tonight. That will help."

My stomach knotted even through my joy. "But . . . they look brand-new. Did you . . ."

I'd had to tell Signora Benucci only yesterday that I wasn't sure when I would be able to buy pointe shoes. I couldn't ask Mom for the money to buy them, and even if I could, I wasn't sure we'd be able to afford them anyway. And now here was Signora Benucci, giving me a pair of pointe shoes that were exactly my size?

"What nonsense!" Signora Benucci clucked her tongue. "I found them in our supply closet, barely used. Someone must have left them here some time ago." It wasn't coincidence, I knew; it was a kindness. Only I didn't know how or when I'd be able to repay her. "Now go ... *prontissimo!*" She clapped and turned away, signaling the end of the discussion.

• • • • • • •

I practically ran all the way to Once upon a Scoop, smiling every time I thought about my beautiful shoes. I burst through the back door of the kitchen, dying to show them off. Then I froze, remembering. I couldn't show them off. At least, not to Mom. I'd have to keep them from her. My stomach fell. Another secret.

"Malic, is that you?" Mom called from out front. A second later, she stuck her head around the door. "I can't find the latest inventory list. Mr. Sneeves said he dropped it off earlier today. Take a quick look in the back office and bring it out if you find it?"

"Sure."

In the back office, I found stacks of papers and receipts, but no inventory list. I opened the bottom drawer of the desk and scanned the files, and when I opened the last one, my heart stopped. There was a stack of job applications, each with dates from the last few days, each with the job listing for "Store Manager" written across the top.

This could only mean one thing: Mr. Sneeves was interviewing people to replace Mom. Anger brought heat to my face. How could he do this to her? She hadn't even had a chance to make any changes to the parlor yet. I gripped the file, pulling it from the drawer.

"No inventory list back here!" I called to Mom. Then I hurried into the kitchen and shoved the file into my schoolbag. Maybe Mr. Sneeves would think he misplaced it. I didn't know if it would stall the process, but hopefully, it would buy us some time.

"*Buongiorno!*"

I jumped, startled, and fell back against Lanz. He caught me, laughing. His arms around my waist sucked the air right out of my lungs. *No no no no*, I scolded myself. This could not keep happening.

"Lanz." I stepped away. "You startled me." I made myself sound way more irritated than I actually felt. If the best offense was a good defense, then my defenses were going up. Way, way up.

His smiled wavered with his surprise. "But . . . what is wrong?"

"Nothing," I grumbled. "I'm fine."

He laid his hand on my arm. "No," he said quietly. "I don't believe you are."

I tried a glare and failed miserably. I wanted to be angry with him, to push him away. But it was impossible. His expression was too open, too cute, too . . . everything. "I just . . . ," I started, feeling a storm of frustration building. "I'm just sick of this place! Of working here!" I threw up my hands. "I hate the ice cream, the customers. All of it!"

He raised one adorably crooked eyebrow. "You hate ice cream?" The corners of his lips slowly curled upward. "I do not think so."

"Fine." I blew out an exasperated breath. "I don't hate it. But . . . I hate what it does to my mom. How she spends every waking minute here and then loses sleep over it at night."

Lanz sat down on one of the metal stools by the ice cream maker and motioned for me to do the same. "Tell me."

I hesitated, feeling like I was standing on the precipice of something big. But Lanz kept looking at me, waiting, his dark, sincere eyes never leaving mine. *Ethan*, I pleaded as I teetered at the edge. Why couldn't Ethan be here right now? Safe, constant Ethan. But Ethan, I knew, was staying late at school to work on his invention.

I took a deep breath, and started talking. Maybe a few minutes passed, or an hour. I didn't know. At some point, a steady rain started falling. I could hear it tap-dancing on the roof over our heads, and I was thankful. Rain like this meant fewer customers. I heard the bell out front jingle half a dozen times, but that was no big deal. Mom stayed up front to handle the orders, which meant I could tell Lanz everything without her overhearing.

I told him what was going on with the parlor, and what Mr. Sneeves had said to Mom about needing to bring in more business. I told him about the job applications I'd found. And I told him how much I worried about Mom and her happiness, how she tried so hard not to let on that she was struggling.

"I want to help her," I said, "but I'm not sure how."

Lanz stayed silent for a long minute, and then smiled. "Gelato."

I blinked. "Huh?"

"We will add gelato to the menu!" Lanz was already moving around the kitchen, grabbing eggs and milk from the refrigerator, and sifting through the fresh fruits and spices that sat on the counter. I hadn't noticed until just then how, over the last few days, the parlor's kitchen had been filling with Lanz's fresh ingredients. Now that I thought about it, I realized that each day he'd brought in some lemons from the farmers' market, or a coconut from one of the trees outside his apartment building. Slowly but surely, he'd been transforming our kitchen. "We'll start with vanilla," he said with decisiveness.

"But we already have vanilla ice cream. Isn't vanilla gelato kind of . . . basic?"

Lanz stared at me, his mouth agape. Then he let loose a

string of Italian that, even though I couldn't understand a word, sounded a lot like ranting. "Basic!" He practically spat the word. "Do you call a grand *jeté* basic? Or a *tombé*?"

"No way," I scoffed.

"Because it is *art*!" He deftly measured milk and cream into a saucepan. "There is nothing basic about gelato. Five hundred years, gelato has existed! It was invented for the court of the great Medicis. My great-great-great-grandfather passed this recipe down to his son, and then to his son after him, and so on and so on . . ." His eyes gleamed with pride. "Until my father passed it on to me. It is a tradition."

He looked so uncharacteristically serious, I suddenly felt the urge to laugh. And then . . . I was laughing. "I'm sorry," I hiccuped. "It's just . . . for a second, I thought you were going to tell me that if I ever shared your secret recipe with anyone, you'd have to kidnap me . . . or something."

He only smiled at that, making my cheeks burn hotter. Then he handed me what looked like a charcoal-colored snap pea. "Smell."

I hesitantly lifted the bean to my nose and breathed in. The silky-smooth scent of vanilla flooded over me. "Yum."

He nodded toward the saucepan. "Into the pot."

I dropped it in, and within minutes, the liquid began to simmer. Lanz scooped out the vanilla bean and opened the pod, scraping the seeds back into the pan, then throwing away the pod shell. We added eggs, just like we had when we'd made ice cream before, only Lanz put in fewer eggs and less cream.

"Less fat means more flavor," Lanz explained. "And we churn it more slowly than ice cream, too, so less air gets into the mixture. But before we do that, we strain the custard." He poured the custard slowly through the strainer in the sink. "This makes the texture smooth and creamy."

When the custard was ready, we set it in the refrigerator. While we waited for it to chill, we worked on Lanz's English reading. The rain kept falling, and the shop stayed quiet. Before I knew it, Mom was closing up for the night.

"We've been making gelato, and it's still got a few more minutes left to churn," I told Mom when she came into the kitchen.

Suddenly, I realized I was reluctant to leave. For the first time in years, I actually wanted to stay at Once upon a Scoop. "Lanz and I will finish it, and I'll meet you at home after? Go relax, Mom! Take a bubble bath."

"A bubble bath," she repeated, like she'd forgotten there was such a thing. "That sounds amazing." She looked from one of us to the other. "Okay. Make sure you lock the door again on your way out. Keep your cell on." She kissed me and waved to Lanz. Then she was gone.

A few minutes later, the gelato finished churning. I grabbed an ice cream scoop, but Lanz placed his hand over mine. "Never use a scoop with gelato." He produced a special paddle from one of the bags he'd brought with him. "Always *una pagaia*." He dipped the paddle into the thick, creamy cloud of gelato and dished us up a big bowl to share.

"Let's try eating it out front," I suggested, grabbing spoons for us. "We can pretend we're customers." We walked out into the parlor, and I gasped. Outside the shop's windows, we could see a fiery pink-and-gold sunset. "Look at that. The rain's finished."

"Let's eat outside," Lanz suggested. "Gelato is always served at a warmer temperature than ice cream. The beach will be the perfect place for it."

"The sand's going to be wet from the rain," I protested.

"Isn't sand always wet?" Lanz laughed. "That is the whole point."

Really, it wasn't the sand, it was the idea. Sunset, beach, boy. A not-Ethan boy. *Oh boy.*

I locked up the shop and Lanz carried the bowl of gelato and our spoons to the beach. When we reached the sand, he slipped off his Vans and I kicked off my flats. We found a spot to sit that was relatively dry. The sun had dipped below the horizon, casting the last of its glittering golds onto the water. Only a few people milled about in the distance.

"Well. Aren't you going to try it?" Lanz asked, nodding to the gelato. Before I could protest, he lifted the spoon to my mouth.

Rich, satiny vanilla ribboned over my tongue with almost impossible softness. "It's like eating a cloud," I murmured, "but the flavor's so . . . intense."

"My father says that ice cream is a nice first date. But gelato . . . gelato is love at first sight."

I kept my eyes glued to the water, not daring to glance his way.

Then he pointed to the waves and whispered, "*Delfini!* Look!"

The fins broke the surface a hundred yards from shore—a pod of dolphins frolicking in the white caps.

"They're *bellissimi*. Beautiful." Lanz followed their path through the waves with his eyes.

"Yes. They are." I scooped another creamy spoonful from the bowl. "It's funny, but the whole time I've worked at the parlor, I've never eaten ice cream—or gelato—" I grinned. "On the beach."

"But why?" he asked. "In Verona, there is no ocean. But if there were . . ." He smiled. "It is hard to think of working at all when a view like that is before you." He gestured to the expanse of ocean.

"I never thought about it that way." I dug my toes into the cool sand. "I'm surrounded by tourists all day long, but I'm so used to living here I don't always see how pretty it is."

"So. Maybe you take time for it more often now."

"That's . . . not easy for me." I shrugged. "I have tunnel vision. A lot of times all I can think about is dance."

"And . . . changing your mind is not easy for you, either."

"What do you mean?"

He studied the sand, seeming uncharacteristically shy. "I have been waiting for you to change your mind. About me."

My heart slammed into my throat. "What? I—I'm not sure I understand."

He brushed a hand through his hair. "You do." He shook his head. "You don't want to like me. I am trying to learn why."

Agh. Why wasn't this simpler? "Lanz. It's—"

"The joking. I know."

I was blushing furiously now. Talk about awkward. "No . . . no. It's not the joking. You catch me off guard. It's distracting, and I don't let myself get distracted. Ever."

"So. You want me to thank you, then? For not ignoring me entirely?"

I flopped back in the sand, laughing. "I give up! You're impossible!"

He grinned. "A compliment from you at last."

I rolled my eyes and sat up. "Will you let me say this?" He made the motion of zipping his lip. "Thank you. So here's the thing. I never thought I'd like working in the parlor again, but since you started helping . . . it's been fun. And . . ." I smiled. "I got pointe shoes today!"

"You did?" He beamed. "*Fantastico!*"

"It feels amazing. And it's because of you. Introducing me to your mom and everything. A lot has happened because of you." I gulped down my nerves and pushed on. "Which is why I, um, I need to tell you I'm sorry. You've been nothing but friendly to me, and I've been—" I dropped my eyes. "Well, I don't think I've been very welcoming."

He leaned closer, until one of his curls brushed against my forehead. "Until today. Maybe you've decided you can like me after all?"

I knew what he meant. He meant friend "like." Of course he did. He was sitting so near to me, though. Suddenly, my head was swimming. Maybe it was the warmth of the sand, or the humidity in the air, or the simple fact that it was the first time I'd ever been so close-up to any boy other than Ethan. Whatever the cause, I understood why I'd been keeping him at a distance. Lanz made me feel things that no one else ever had before. Scary, surprising things. Enticing things. I didn't know what to do with that, or what it meant.

"Maybe I can," I whispered.

Chapter Eight

"You better not be feeding me *formiche*, or anything else in the insect family." I started to lift the edge of the blindfold, but Lanz grabbed my hand and placed it firmly in my lap.

"No peeking for the taste test." His scolding tone held a note of laughter. It was Sunday, and we'd come to the parlor an hour earlier than usual so we'd have quiet time for this.

"You use your sense of taste and smell only," Lanz continued. "The best way to select flavors, my father says, is with feeling. And for your information, pistachio gelato with chocolate-covered crickets is delicious. I tasted it myself at the international gelato festival last year. But . . ." I could hear his smile. "Since *you* are faint of heart, no bugs for you today. Instead . . ."

I heard the clinking of a spoon, and then a strong but welcome scent wafted under my nose. "Licorice," I guessed.

"Good." He held the spoon to my mouth. "Now taste."

The rich licorice ice cream zinged over my tongue, but there was another more delicate flavor. "Is that a flower?"

"Violets," Lanz said, sounding impressed. "Now for another ice cream."

A creamy, chocolate scent filled my nose. "*Yum.* That's a yes already." I opened my mouth and tasted mellow hazelnut mingled with richer, bittersweet chocolate. "Delicious. What is it?"

"An ice cream called Baci," he said. "Italian, for *kisses.*"

"What?" a familiar voice said. I yanked off my blindfold. Ethan stood in the doorway of the parlor's kitchen.

I dropped my hands, sure my face was glowing. I scrambled up from the stool I'd been sitting on. "Lanz was just testing some new flavors out on me." I frantically grabbed a sponge to clean off the counter and made myself look extremely busy.

Ethan looked back and forth between Lanz and me, his face thoughtful and serious. How long had he been standing there? A nervous flutter struck up in my stomach. What could he be thinking?

"Hey, you." Finally, Ethan smiled and reached for my hand.

"Hey yourself." As my fingers brushed his, the universe righted itself, and the simple comfort of his hand in mine washed away the dizzying bewilderment I'd felt only a few minutes before.

"Ethan." Lanz clapped him on the shoulder, then said, "It is VIP time, yes?" It hadn't taken long for Lanz to fall into our morning hang-time mix. Now he pushed through the kitchen doors, offering cheerful hellos to Tilly and Andres, who were already waiting at our table.

"Do you feel okay?" Ethan asked me. "Your face is red."

"Is it?" I said offhandedly. "It's hot outside." Except I hadn't been outside for the last hour. *Nice one, Malie.* We stood in silence, neither one of us seeming to know what to say. Weird. I couldn't think of a time when we'd run out of things to say to each other before.

I was guiltily relieved when Tilly stuck her head around the door to break our conversational deadlock. "You guys hanging with us or what? Your mom's already opening the shop, and if you don't hurry, she's going to rope you into work."

Ethan and I left the kitchen and joined our friends at the table by the front window. Andres, I saw, had already polished off a banana split. I laughed and rolled my eyes at him, and within seconds, I felt the in-sync-ness of our group again. Phew. Back to normalcy.

"Okay, peeps, we have a new mission," Tilly announced. "Find Lanz a date."

Or not.

"Tilly, *per favore*—" Lanz laughed, his cheeks flushing.

I coughed. "What?"

Tilly stared at each of us in turn, as if she couldn't believe we could be so oblivious. "For the school's spring carnival? It's in two weeks. We go with dates, ergo, Lanz needs a date."

"*Va bene*, Tilly. I am fine without a date." Lanz met my eyes for a millisecond and then he looked away. "I don't even know what this spring carnival is."

"Basically a school-wide beach party," Andres said as he dove into a second sundae. "It's at the Marina Springs pier. There are games and rides. A surfing contest. It's a blast."

"Except when you're stuck scooping ice cream," I said. "I have to work the Once upon a Scoop booth."

"Not this year," Tilly said. "Don't even *think* about ditching us. You talk to your mom, or I will."

I swear, if Mom hadn't just disappeared into the kitchen, Tilly would've already started in on her.

"*I'll* talk to Mom, but I'm not holding my breath." I hated watching the carnival from the sidelines, but with Mom's stress level in the red zone, I didn't have much hope of her relenting. "If I don't go, then Ethan and Lanz can hang out, and Lanz won't need a date." I felt a mysterious relief as I said it.

"But . . . Tilly's right," Lanz said. "You should come, Malie."

"See?" Tilly nudged me. "It's unanimous. You're coming. So. Lanz. Date." She scanned the parlor, looking for prospective candidates among the dozen or so kids from school hanging out there. It was a cloudless day with record-breaking heat, and it seemed like half the town had decided to head for the beach. Of course, everyone was getting ice cream first.

"I know somebody," Ethan said. "Eve Hunter. She's one of the Invention Convention kids. She's great—funny, smart." He turned to Lanz. "I can introduce you."

"I didn't know you knew Eve." I glanced at Ethan in surprise. "She's in my bio class."

Ethan shrugged. "Sometimes we're in the lab at the same time. Anyway, Lanz, what do you say?"

"If Lanz said he doesn't want a date, he doesn't want one," I said. "Don't push him into it." Every eye at the table turned to me, questioning. Why had I just said that? What was it to me if Lanz asked someone to the carnival? I wished that somebody would change the subject. This whole date confab was getting on my nerves.

A second later, Lanz broke the silence. "*Sí.* Yes, I will meet this Eve. If she likes, I will take her to the carnival. Only . . . there is a problem. What if she doesn't want to go with me?"

"She will," we all said together. We'd all seen the way girls looked at Lanz as they passed him in school. Even now there was a group of girls eyeing him over their milk shakes, giggling and whispering to each other. His personality and his smile were infectious, and he had the accent working in his favor. There wasn't a single girl who would've said no to Lanz Benucci.

My stomach flipped at the thought. I stood suddenly. "You guys figure it out. I have to get some toppings from the kitchen."

Ethan stood, too, giving me a peck on the cheek. "I'm heading out. Lanz, I'll introduce you to Eve on Monday."

Lanz nodded. "*Grazie*."

As I walked to the kitchen, Tilly dropped into step beside me, her eagle eyes scoping my face.

"Spill it."

"I don't know what you're talking about," I said lightly.

"What was that weirdness over the whole Lanz-bringing-a-date thing?" She stuck her hand on her hip. The goddess braids crowning her head added to her no-nonsense demeanor. "We're talking about the carnival, not an arranged marriage."

"I was not being weird!" I protested as I poured fresh blueberries into a metal display bin. "I just think it's ridiculous to force him to ask somebody. I mean, if there was a girl he was interested in...fine. But shouldn't it happen more... organically?"

Tilly snorted. "Look who's talking. If Andres and I hadn't coupled up, you and Ethan never would've gotten together. Your first kiss only happened because you guys got so bored watching *us* kiss." As if on cue, Andres snuck up behind Tilly and tickled her waist. She squealed and ducked away from him.

I stiffened. "It wasn't that predictable." Only...had it been? I remembered the awkwardness I'd felt when Tilly and Andres had taken their friendship to the flirt level, and how many times Ethan and I had ended up as a twosome, more by default than by chemistry.

"All I'm saying," Tilly went on, "is that you two didn't happen organically, but look how it turned out. You're two peas in a pod. You couldn't be any more alike if you tried."

I felt oddly unsettled by her words. The way she described

Ethan and me, our relationship sounded about as exciting as a pair of worn socks. Was that the way it was supposed to be? Ethan was my first and only boyfriend, so I didn't have much else to go on. Except for Tilly and Andres. I glanced at them now. Andres had his arm slung loosely around Tilly's shoulder while she scrolled through her phone. He smiled down at her in this half-adoring, half-amused way. Every few seconds, she'd nudge him playfully with her shoulder.

"You're right. He should ask someone." I said it partially because I wanted the conversation to be over, and partially because to say anything different would've been nosing into Lanz's business more than I had any right to. "It's a good thing," I added, with as much conviction as I could.

Tilly rolled her eyes. "One minute Miss Negativity, the next Miss Matchmaker. Mal, do me a favor. Next time the cray-crays come knocking, don't answer."

I laughed and headed into the kitchen. A few minutes later when Lanz came back to start a new batch of lemon gelato, I found myself casting glances in his direction, wondering what he was thinking about. Or who. Had he had a girlfriend before in Italy? If so, what had she been like? Probably laid-back, with a great sense of humor, like Lanz. Nothing like studious Eve. Or—I thought with a sinking feeling—like me.

• • • • • • •

I crossed the floor in a series of *bourrées*, keeping my ankles as tightly knit as possible while taking the tiny steps on pointe.

"Lift your chest," Signora Benucci said. "As if you are a puppet with a string at the center of your rib cage."

I pulled my rib cage upward, tightening my abdomen to support my posture.

"Strong ankles . . . and where is your weight? Not in the back. Centered. Centered."

I'd been on pointe for two weeks now, and I was slowly getting used to the redistribution of weight on my toes and arches. In a way, I felt like I was relearning every position. *Step, step, step, lift, lift, lift.* I tried to ignore the pain in my toes. They were throbbing, but I hardly cared.

Dancing pointe brought me one step closer to dancing professionally someday. I had a long road before me, and knowing that only made me want to work harder.

Now Signora Benucci clapped her hands, signaling the end of today's lessons.

"How are your feet?" she inquired as I slipped off my pointe shoes.

At home, I'd broken in the toe boxes by crushing and bending them against the floor and my hands. Then I'd fitted the shoes with gel toe pads and sewed on the ankle ribbons. I'd been adjusting them over and over again until they felt right. Over time, I knew, I would learn how to customize each pair I owned, but with this first pair, it was trial and error.

"They're all right," I said to Signora Benucci, trying not to wince as I put on my street shoes.

She smiled knowingly. "It will get easier. You're progressing nicely." Then she shook her finger at me. "Don't let what I just said blow your head into a balloon."

I nodded, then paused, not wanting to ask the question burning in my chest, but knowing I had to. "Signora Benucci, the auditions for *Cinderella* are next week, and—" I stopped, too nervous to continue.

"You're wondering if you might audition." Her eyes bored into mine, and I held my breath, waiting. "I spoke to the board of directors. It wasn't an easy task, but because you were already a long-time student here, they agreed to let you audition."

"Really?" Relief made me giddy. "I can't believe it! Thank you so much." Then a worrying thought struck me. "Are you sure I'm ready?"

"Malie, I wouldn't have asked the board to make an exception in the first place if I wasn't confident in your abilities. You will be as prepared for the auditions as any other student here."

"But my pointe technique—"

"Is still being refined," she finished for me. "The same is true of all the other dancers here who've just begun pointe. The judges are aware of that. And the principal role in *Cinderella* has been choreographed with that in mind."

"I'll practice as much as it takes."

She nodded. "I am only one of five judges on the audition panel. I cannot promise you anything."

"Of course." I understood how these things worked. But if only I knew how I compared to everyone else.

"Don't think about other dancers," Signora Benucci said, as if she could read my mind. "Think what *you* can show the judges."

She disappeared into her office, leaving me in the studio, alone with my frustration. I thought about the hours and hours I'd spent in this studio over the past couple weeks, while Mom thought I was meeting Tilly for project prep. I fell asleep exhausted each night, only to dream of dance. Would it make a difference?

I walked out of the studio, lost in my thoughts. I didn't see the figure standing in the hallway until I nearly collided with her.

It was Violet Olsen, peering down at me with her sharp, cat-like eyes.

"Malie!" Her gaze flitted to the pointe shoes dangling from my hand. "What a shocker! I had no idea you were still dancing here. I was watching you."

"You were?" I glanced at the studio door, suddenly wishing the window cutout wasn't there. Of all the people to see me here, it had to be her?

Since I'd quit our ballet class, I'd only seen Violet in passing at school, hoping to avoid any prying questions. Only once, she came up to me in the cafeteria and said, "I'm so bummed to lose my dance buddy." Uh-huh. Sure she was.

Now Violet smiled appreciatively. "Your pointe needs work, but A for the effort. Ice cream's more your thing, don't you think?"

I bristled. "Not at all, actually. It's always been dance for me."

"Huh." Violet nodded. "So this is why you quit our class? To take private lessons with Signora Benucci? I'd love to know how you managed that."

I shrugged. "She offered to teach me."

Violet's eyes darkened, but her smile remained unwavering. "Strange. My parents wanted me to take classes privately, but Signora Benucci told them her schedule was too busy."

My cheeks flushed. I had to be careful in my reaction. "I don't really know how it happened. Maybe she ended up with some free time after all?"

"Mmm. Maybe." Violet's smile widened, which made me even more worried. "Maybe my mom can call your mom? Your mom could fill her in on the details."

"No!" My panicked voice echoed in the room. More students were filing in for the afternoon's classes now. The more people who saw me here, the greater the chance word would get around to my mom that I was taking lessons. Dread filled me. "I mean," I quickly added, "I actually haven't told my mom about the lessons yet. My dad set them up for me to help me get ready for the *Cinderella* audition."

Violet's eyes widened. "Wait. You're still auditioning? I didn't think you could if you weren't officially enrolled in a group class?" Her mouth was a thin line of barely masked annoyance.

"I'm not sure how it worked out," I improvised. I didn't feel comfortable telling her about the exception that had been made for me. "And the thing is, if I make it, it will be a great surprise for Mom. She's been stressed lately. I thought it would cheer her up." *Aue*. Oh no. I was digging a deeper and deeper hole.

"A surprise for sure," Violet said. She put her hand on my shoulder and squeezed gently, as if she were being a supportive bestie. "It's so cute that you have such spirit. I know we're going to need a whole troop of mice. You'd look adorbs in whiskers."

"Thanks," I said through clenched teeth. "I'll be glad to have any part."

Violet nodded. "Always a good idea not to set your expectations too high. Though I'm pretty much a shoo-in for Cinderella."

"How do you know?"

"Oh, Signora Benucci's hinted," she said offhandedly. "Not officially. I have to audition. Protocol and all." She tipped her head down. "Anyway, everyone deserves a fair chance. I wouldn't feel right about being the principal ballerina if I hadn't earned it."

"No. I'm sure you wouldn't." I had my backpack in a death grip now. "I should get going." I turned for the door, then paused. "Um, could you please not say anything to my mom about seeing me here, or my lessons?"

"Absolutely! I'd never do anything to spoil your surprise." She pressed a finger to her lips. "Sealed."

"Thanks," I said as I let myself out. I tried not to dwell on my run-in with Violet, but dread shadowed me for the whole walk. I didn't trust her, and now she was privy to my biggest secret. So. Not. Good.

Chapter Nine

"I'm here!" I called, opening the back door to the kitchen. Mom was going to be seriously peeved that I was late. I'd tried to hurry, but my toes were so sore from ballet that my walk had turned into a hobble. "Sorry I'm la—"

My words were lost in the sound of singing. Mom's singing. I stopped, frozen. Mom was stirring cookie bits into a container of soft, freshly made ice cream. And ... she was singing. Bon Jovi's "You Give Love a Bad Name." Her hips swayed to the rhythm, and she smiled to herself as she stirred.

"Mom?"

She jumped, then looked up at me sheepishly. "Oh, Malie. I didn't hear you."

"Obviously." I laughed, stepping inside. "*Somebody's* in a good mood."

Mom quit stirring to grab me in a spontaneous hug. "You're not going to believe what happened. Mr. Sneeves stopped by a few minutes ago."

"Wait." I pulled away from her, pressing a hand to her forehead. "Mom, do you have a fever? Are you actually *happy* he stopped by?"

Mom giggled. "He told me he was impressed, *keiki*! He used that word. 'Impressed.' Our sales have doubled in the last two weeks. Can you believe it?"

"No . . ."

Mom dipped a tasting spoon into the ice cream and held it out to me. "It's the flavors Lanz is coming up with, and his gelatos. Yesterday's new flavor was honey lavender, today it's Cartellata. Here. Try."

I slid the spoon into my mouth. Cinnamon cookie bits interspersed with honey-flavored gelato. "That's flawless."

"I know!" Mom snapped the lid onto the container. "Honestly, I wasn't sure about Lanz's ideas, but the customers can't get enough of his flavors. And our catering orders have doubled, too. Having Lanz's help has made all the difference."

"That's great." I squeezed Mom's hand. Her eyes were bright. She looked relaxed for the first time in weeks.

She slipped an arm around my shoulders. "I've been thinking about the school carnival, too. It's tomorrow night, isn't it?"

I nodded. I'd mentioned it to her once, but when she had given me her usual, "I'm sorry, but I don't think you're going to be able to go" spiel, I'd let it drop.

"You don't have to remind me," I said now. "I know we're going to have to work late."

She brushed at a strand of hair that had come loose from my ponytail. "*Not* what I was going to say." Her smile widened. "I was going to say that since things are running so smoothly with the parlor, and we're ahead in our monthly sales already, I can spare you tomorrow night. If you still want to go to the carnival, that is?" Her eyes twinkled.

"Really?" When she nodded, I hugged her until she laughed

and cried for mercy. "Thanks, Mom! This is going to be so great. I can't wait to tell Lanz!"

She blinked, giving me a curious look. "You mean Ethan?"

"Oh!" I slapped my forehead. "Yes! Ethan!" How had Lanz's name slipped out? "I'm going to text him right now." I pulled out my phone.

As my thumbs flew over the keys, Mom continued, "Do you see now what a good thing it is that you quit dance? The shop's doing better. You have free time for your school project with Tilly *and* for fun with your friends."

My thumbs froze. I hated that I was lying to her, still. "Mom, the fact that things are better has nothing to do with me quitting dance," I said. Maybe I could somehow steer the conversation to the truth . . .

"But you've been able to focus your energies elsewhere, and it's made a difference." She looked thoughtful, and suddenly, a little sad. "I know what it's like to waste moments wishing for something that can never be. It's not a healthy way to live."

"You're talking about you and Dad now. That's totally different than my dancing."

"Why?" she asked. "I loved your father and wanted him to be someone he couldn't be. You love dance and wanted it to grow into something it couldn't."

"Mom . . ." *I should tell her everything*, I thought. *Prove to her how wrong she is.* But I couldn't. I was afraid she'd refuse to let me audition for *Cinderella*, or worse, that she'd forbid me from dancing forever. And we were finally getting to a better place, Mom and I. Now I didn't want to ruin things with an argument.

I turned away, grabbing the Cartellata gelato from the counter. "I'll put this in the deep freeze, and then see if Lanz needs help out front." I mustered up a smile, then kissed her cheek. "And thanks for the carnival. I'm super excited to go!"

Mom took up humming again. I vowed to shake off her words about dance and focus on what was happening here and now. Mom was happy, and I loved seeing her this way. I stepped inside the freezer, then paused, taking in the towers of containers rising before me. The freezer was twice as full as it had been before Lanz started working here. It was stacked with flavors that Lanz had invented—Peter Panforte, Rumpeltwixkin,

Licorice Red Riding Hood, Bibbity-Bobbity-Mou. Many were blended with Italian candies and chocolate, such as the toffee-like *mou* I'd tried and loved. I'd been so consumed with my lessons at the conservatory, I hadn't noticed the transformation taking place right under my very nose.

I left the freezer and eased the swinging door to the front of the parlor open, peeking in.

"*Buon pomeriggio*, Madison!" Lanz cried as a little girl ran into the shop, her black curls and bathing suit covered in sand. He bowed to her and then took her hand, letting her twirl underneath his arm as he said hello to her parents. "Have you come for your Principessa Struffoli sundae?" She nodded, and he breezed behind the counter, grabbing a sundae tray with a flourish. "*Va bene*, are you ready?"

He curled a heaping scoop of the Italian-cookie-filled ice cream onto the scooper, then launched it catapult-style into the air, spun around, and caught it in the sundae bowl behind his back. Madison squealed with delight. He wasn't just making a sundae, he was giving a performance. When he finished, every customer in the shop applauded.

Lanz turned back to the counter, catching sight of me.

"Spying on me, eh?"

"No." Heat rushed to my cheeks.

He raised an eyebrow. "You are a terrible liar." I took two steps into the parlor, and Lanz cocked his head to one side, watching me. "And . . . you're hurting."

"It's nothing." I lowered my voice so Mom wouldn't hear. "My feet are sore from the pointe shoes. That's all."

He glanced down at my feet, concern crinkling his brow.

I brushed past him to take the order of the next customer in line. "I need to keep practicing. The auditions are only—"

"Six days away," Lanz finished for me. "I know, Malie. I pay attention."

"You have to," I said, scooping some *panna cotta* ice cream into a cone for a high schooler in a wet suit. "Because of your mom."

"I don't have to," he said quietly. "I want to. Because it's important to you." Warmth stirred inside me, and I started to turn away, but he stopped me.

"You're always trying to run away. Have you noticed? I

wonder sometimes if you believe dance is all you need. Nothing else. No one else."

"I don't think that. I have Ethan, Tilly, Andres. And—" I stopped just short of adding *you*, not knowing how he might respond.

He paused over the cone he was scooping. "And me, I hope?"

"Of course. You too," I added, flustered. He studied my face with that quizzical expression he seemed to reserve just for me. That look had grown familiar over the past weeks of working side by side. Even so, it set my pulse flickering every time.

"You know, you make me think of two customers who visit my father's gelateria each Friday. An old woman and her pet potbellied pig, Porcini."

I snorted. "You're kidding."

Lanz shook his head. "No. This is truth." He loved to tell me stories about Italy and his dad's shop, but a potbellied pig? This was a first. "This woman buys ten gallons of pistachio gelato every week for this pig. When my father once asked her why, she said it was to console the pig. Because Porcini dreams of being a cow."

I burst out laughing. "Wait a sec. If you tell me I'm the pig in this story, I'll dump ice cream on your head."

"Never." He grinned impishly. "But Papa likes to get on his knees before Porcini. He says, 'Porcini, the life of a gelato-eating pig is a fine life. Let it be enough.'" He looked at me with one eyebrow raised, until I nudged his shoulder.

"What?"

He nudged me back. "Sometimes, you can let now be enough."

I paused over his words, my scoop in my hand. *Now*. What was happening *now*?

Now Mom's smile was resurfacing for the first time in I couldn't even remember how long, and I realized how much Lanz had to do with that.

I thought about telling him that, but soon a flurry of customers were rushing in, and there was no chance for any more talking. My feet ached as the hours passed. As the sun began to set and many of the customers headed off, Mom came out of the kitchen smiling (again!).

"You must have made a hundred sundaes today," she said to us.

"More." I leaned against the counter.

"I'll close up tonight," she said. "You two have homework to do, or Instagram pics to post, or *something* better to do." Lanz started to protest, but she waved us both away. "Go on. Get out of here."

"You don't have to tell *me* twice," I replied, then ducked as she threw a hand towel at my head.

Lanz and I grabbed our schoolbags and stepped outside. The evening had cooled to the perfect temperature—warm but not hot, with a salt-infused breeze blowing in from the ocean.

"So . . . are you heading to the beach?" I asked Lanz. "Tilly texted me. She and Andres are down by the cove surfing."

"What are you doing?" Lanz asked me.

"I need to go home and rest my feet," I said. "Pretty fun, huh?"

"Well, it can be fun," Lanz argued, his eyes sparkling. "Do you mind if I join you? I could even help."

"Really?" I asked, mystified but too happy to say no.

• • • • • • •

Twenty minutes later, Lanz set a large, steaming bowl at my feet. He'd taken over our kitchen, rummaging through cabinets until he found a bowl and the salt, and then he'd made me sit at the table while he prepared a warm salt bath.

"It just needs one more thing," he said, digging through his messenger bag. He produced a Ziploc bag full of tiny purple seeds. "Lavender. I had some left over from the ice cream I made yesterday." He poured the lavender into his hand, then crushed it between his palms, sprinkling it into the bowl. "It will help with the soreness."

"You're an expert," I teased.

He smiled. "My mom was a professional dancer. My father used to do this for her when her feet were sore. Back when things were still good between them."

I blushed. The fact that his dad had done this for his mom imbued the whole thing with a sort of romantic undertone. Then I blushed all over again, telling myself that I was reading too much into a simple act of kindness.

The sweet smell of lavender drifted over me. I set my bare

feet ever so gently into the warm water. Then I leaned back in the chair, every muscle unwinding.

Lanz sat in the chair beside me. "You should be kinder to yourself," he said. "You push and push, without rest."

"I have to." My voice sounded so relaxed that I couldn't even muster a legitimately argumentative tone.

"Not all the time." He tilted his head at me.

"I guess not," I relinquished. "Lanz?" My heart hammered with what I knew I wanted to say. "That story you told me today? I'm not Porcini. Hanging out with my friends, hanging out with you . . . is enough."

He glanced at me, a slow smile spanning his face. "Thank you." Two burgundy spots appeared on the apples of his cheeks, and my pulse began racing. I had the sense that something huge was about to happen. "I'm glad we're friends now, too. It took long enough, but it happened." He grinned, but this time there was a nervous vibe between us that made the joking miss the mark. "But, Mal, I think—"

My cell phone buzzed. I pulled it from my back pocket to see a text from Ethan.

Hey, you. Got ur message about the carnival. Great news! We've both been so busy lately. Will be good to catch up.

I blinked, reality settling over me full force. Ethan. I was going to the carnival with Ethan. Which was good. No . . . great! But . . . I was sitting alone in my kitchen with Lanz. Which was . . . What was it? What was this? And what had he been about to say to me?

"What is it?" Lanz asked me.

"Oh." I laughed awkwardly. "Just a text from Ethan. I told him I could go to the carnival. Mom decided to let me go."

Lanz nodded. "I hoped she would."

"Wait . . . what?"

He shrugged. "I might have suggested that you deserved a break. One time, or . . . maybe ten times. That's all."

I laughed. "I can't believe it. So I suppose I should be thanking you for that, too!" I rolled my eyes, trying to make it seem like all these thank-yous were getting old.

"No thanks needed. Really, I was being selfish." His eyes locked on mine. "You would have been missed."

I swallowed, not knowing where to look. He didn't mean *he'd* miss me. He couldn't mean that. Only . . . why did it sound like he did?

"Not that much," I said quickly. "Ethan's used to not having me go. And Tilly and Andres will be glued to each other all night long." Then I stiffened, remembering. "And . . . you're going with Eve Hunter, right?"

Lanz nodded with an air of surprise, as if he'd only just remembered. "*Sí*. I don't know anything about her, but Ethan has many nice things to say."

"He does?" I asked.

"He says she's clever, and funny. And . . . how did he say it? Oh yes. He said she has an adorable laugh."

"Adorable," I repeated. "Huh." Had Ethan ever called me adorable? I thought back. He'd called me driven and single-minded, both of which I'd taken as great compliments. But adorable? Nope. What qualities did Ethan find adorable, and why didn't I know what they were? "Well, if she's that adorable, I'll bet you'll have a great time with her." I meant it kindly, but it came out monotone.

Lanz shrugged. "It's a new experience, and I'll be with friends. This will make it a great time." He gestured to my phone. "You should text Ethan. He'll want to hear from you."

I nodded. "Yeah." Disappointment washed over me. I needed to get back to Ethan, but I wasn't ready for Lanz to leave. I couldn't ask him to stay, though. That would be too weird. And maybe even wrong?

Lanz stood to leave, and I stood, too, almost tipping the bowl of water. "Lanz, wait! You were going to tell me something before. What was it?"

He met my gaze and smiled. It wasn't his usual carefree smile, but one that was serious. "Only that . . . I thank you for your help with my English. And that I admire your . . ." He paused to contemplate the right word. "Ambition. It impresses me."

"Don't be impressed," I said. "If I get a part in *Cinderella*, then that will be something."

His smile shifted from serious to a little sad. "My mother used to say things like that. 'If I can dance in a company, then *that* will be something. If I can be a prima ballerina, then *that* will be something.'" He shook his head. "My father couldn't understand it."

"Why not?" I asked.

"He said that life is full of tremendous moments disguised as ordinary ones. That you don't need to *be* great to live a great life."

"And you agree with him."

"I think you have to balance drive with joyfulness." In an instant, his sober expression was replaced with a mischievous one. "And so, tomorrow, Malie Analu, you will make time for a little joy?"

I smiled. "I will."

Chapter Ten

I popped a piece of cotton candy into my mouth and watched as Tilly picked up another empty popcorn container from the ground. Long lines always kept Tilly busy, because she had so much time to notice the litter.

"You can't pick up every piece of trash, Till," I said over the shrieking coming from the Tilt-A-Whirl. The school carnival stretched down the length of the pier, a parade of colored lights and music. It was brilliant in its chaos and vibrancy. The lines for the rides, though, were endless.

"I can." Tilly mock-glared at me. "I will."

Andres grabbed her waist and spun her around, making her

dissolve into giggles. They kissed, and I turned back to Ethan, Eve, and Lanz. I never felt like an outsider around Andres and Tilly, even though sometimes I could swear they were speaking some language of love that was completely foreign to me. Tonight, though, things felt different.

Lanz, Eve, Ethan, and I made an awkward foursome on the outskirts of Tilly and Andres's seamless couplehood.

"They're so good together," Eve remarked, looking shy.

"They always have been," I said. "Right, Ethan?" I turned to Ethan, but he had his head bent over his phone. "Ethan?"

"Huh?" He blinked, like he was waking up from a dream. "Sorry. What?"

I held back a sigh. This was how the entire night had gone so far. Lanz, who was usually so chatty and comfortable, was strangely quiet around Eve. I felt oddly buoyed by the fact that they weren't hitting it off, and then guilty that I seemed to want their date to fail. It didn't help that Ethan, all the while, had stayed firmly focused on his phone.

Now he smiled apologetically. "I was just rereading my invention log. It has to be ready for the judges by next week."

"But I'm off work," I gently reminded him. "I'm at the carnival for the first time ever. Maybe the invention log can wait?"

He hesitated, then smiled. "You're right. It's gone as of now—"

"Ethan, wait," Eve piped up. "I've been meaning to ask you if I could see your log. I've been having trouble with mine. I'd love to see how yours is coming together."

"Really?" His eyes brightened. If his face hadn't been cast in the shadow of the Tilt-A-Whirl, I swear I might've seen him blushing. "If you really want to . . ." He glanced at me, then added, "It'll just be a minute, Mal. I'll put the phone away afterward. Promise."

He didn't wait for me to respond before he and Eve bent their heads over his phone, lost in some science lingo that only they could understand. They stayed like that until it was finally our turn for the Tilt-A-Whirl.

"She's great, isn't she?" Ethan asked me as we slid into our neon-orange egg-shaped car for the ride.

"Yeah, very sweet. But I'm not sure she and Lanz have much in common." I craned my neck to get a glimpse of them on their shared Tilt-A-Whirl seat. They sat with a generous space between them. Both of them were smiling politely, like they were trying to be good sports. "It's not the worst thing in the world if they end up not being into each other. Right?"

"Right," Ethan seconded. "Lanz isn't much of a science guy, I guess."

"Nope. And she certainly seems into science."

"She lives for it!" Ethan nodded. "Her invention is brilliant, actually. Way more impressive than mine. If she makes it to the national convention, it'll be a blast to go with her." He stopped, then added, "I mean, just to hang out with another kid from our school there, you know?"

I studied his face. I didn't think I'd ever seen him so enthusiastic about anything other than science before. Lit up from the inside out. That was how he looked. A sudden thought struck me: *Does Ethan look like that when he thinks about me? When he talks about me to his friends in science lab?*

Then the ride started, the world whirled, and the thought slipped away into the streams of light spinning around us.

I gripped Ethan's arm, burying my head against his shoulder, and he wrapped his arm around me. I waited to feel an electric rush, but nothing happened except a dizzying headache.

When the ride finished, I climbed out of our car unsteadily and with the bland sensation of being let down, although by what, exactly, I couldn't say. Tilly and Andres were waiting for us, Tilly rolling her eyes at Andres as he pretended to be so dizzy that he had to cling to her for support. Lanz and Eve stood a polite distance apart, quiet and awkward. Eve looked pale, and I wondered if all that spinning had been too much for her.

We bought more cotton candy, then walked to the fun house, which was Andres's favorite.

"You just like to check out your biceps in the hall of mirrors," Tilly teased him.

"How do you know I'm not admiring *you*?" Andres retorted. "Instead of one Tilly, there are dozens."

She made a face, but I could tell she was pleased by what he'd said.

We walked into the fun house, navigating a crooked floor, a

151

maze of doors, and an optical illusion room. Andres and Tilly went up ahead, and Eve and I fell into step beside each other as we entered a narrow corridor of revolving barrels. I leapt lightly over the barrels, but Eve stumbled until we reached the other side. Then she closed her eyes and leaned on the wall.

"Are you okay?" I asked.

She pressed her hands against the wall for support. "I need some fresh air. That spinning ride . . ."

I peered down the next corridor. "There's only the hall of mirrors left to go. Can you make it?"

She glanced back at Lanz and Ethan, who were a few steps behind us.

"Let's go," Eve said. "I don't want to ruin everyone's fun." She stepped into the corridor of seemingly endless mirrors. I followed with the guys close behind, but within seconds, everyone's reflections fractured into a hundred different ones. I turned a slow circle, sure that I'd be able to pick out which Ethan, Eve, or Lanz was real and which was a mirror image. Every face I saw was distorted—too far away, too close—too squat, too long. Then every face disappeared in the mirrors but my own.

"Hello?" I called out. "Ethan? Lanz?"

No answer came.

I tried to get my bearings, then reached out, but my hands only met cold, hard glass. Suddenly, I felt trapped. I walked faster, bumping into mirrored corners, searching for the exit, and then shrieked when I backed into someone. I spun, colliding foreheads with the stranger.

"Malie," a familiar voice whispered. "It's me." Lanz's breath was warm against my ear; his hands rested on my waist. I felt an electric zing. "Are you all right?"

"Y-yes." Lanz's eyes were so near that I could see the subtle shift his irises made from chestnut centers to oaken rims, light to dark. The mirrors around us blurred into a diamond-white shimmer. I'd wanted to leave the corridor seconds before. Now all I could think of was lingering, just to be near him.

"We thought you were outside already," Lanz said softly. "I would've stayed behind if I'd known. Or Ethan would've, I'm sure . . ."

Ethan. Flustered, I stepped back. "Eve wasn't feeling well," I said. "I was with her, but—"

Lanz nodded. "She got lost in the mirrors, too. We all did. But Ethan's outside with her now, getting her some ginger ale." He offered me his hand. "Are you ready?"

I nodded, but didn't take his hand. The same lightning bolt might strike again, and then what? Then ... nothing. He was supposed to be with Eve. I was supposed to be with Ethan. That was all there was to it. "Thanks. I'm fine now."

His hand dropped to his side as a fleeting disappointment crossed his features. But no ... it had to be a trick of the light. We left the fun house in silence, but Lanz glanced in my direction every few seconds. I didn't know if he was making sure I was okay, or if he was trying to puzzle through what I was thinking. Either way, I couldn't meet his eyes.

We found Ethan and Eve sitting side by side on the beach near the pier, watching the waves break on the moonlit water. If I didn't know better, I would've thought *they* were a couple. When Ethan heard us, he leapt up, tripping over his feet to get to me.

"Mal, what happened? We were in the hall of mirrors, and then you were gone."

I waved a dismissive hand. "Just got turned around in there, that's all."

Eve glanced up at me apologetically as she sipped her soda.

"Tilly and Andres are riding the Ferris wheel," Ethan said. "Eve's not up for it."

"I'm sorry, but I need to go home," Eve said. "My mom's picking me up. She'll be waiting in the pier parking lot."

"I'll walk you to the car." Lanz offered her the very hand that mere minutes before he'd offered to me. I felt a pang of jealousy as Eve gratefully slid her hand into his. But, I reminded myself, I already *had* a boyfriend. A very nice boyfriend.

As Lanz and Eve walked toward the parking lot, Ethan and I watched them go in silence.

"We could catch up with Tilly and Andres," he offered. "Ride a few more rides?"

But I could tell his heart wasn't in it. Mine wasn't, either. How many times had I wished in years past that I could come to this carnival instead of working at it? Now I was here, but this night wasn't anything like I'd imagined it would be.

"Why don't you go ahead?" I said to him. "The hall of mirrors did me in, too." I wanted a break. From the rides and—yes—even though I felt awful admitting it to myself, from Ethan.

Ethan shook his head. "I've only got two more days before the convention, and I need to add some final touches to my display." He hugged me, then brushed my lips in a light kiss. There was no bolt of electricity. The memory of Lanz's hand on my waist swept my breath away, and I stepped back from Ethan.

"So you're going home?" he asked.

I hesitated. I didn't want to be alone with my thoughts yet. Not when I couldn't make sense of them. So I said the first thing that popped into my head, the one thing that I wouldn't have said in a million years unless I'd been such an emotional mess that I couldn't see any other solution. "I think I'll see if Mom needs help at the ice cream booth."

• • • • • • •

I glanced at my nightstand clock. It was past eleven, and I couldn't fall asleep. After I'd helped Mom take down the ice cream booth, we'd come back home and Mom had gone straight to bed. I'd been too wired, so I FaceTimed with Dad. It was late afternoon in Oahu and he was selling his paintings. He held up his latest pieces for me to see, and, when he asked about Once upon a Scoop, I told him that business was booming. Maybe it was out of loyalty to Mom, but I felt the need to tell Dad how great she was doing.

"What about ballet?" he asked. "Are you hanging in there without it?"

My stomach clenched. I wasn't a daughter who snuck behind my parents' backs. Ever. And yet . . . here I was, lying to both of them.

"Maybe I'll still get a chance to dance again someday," I said vaguely.

Dad nodded. "You will. I'm sure of it."

We ended our FaceTime session when Dad was approached by a customer. I hung up wondering if all kids of divorce tiptoed around certain touchy subjects like I did. I found myself wanting to ask Lanz about it, which threw me right back into emotional shambles. I pressed my face into my pillow, letting out a muffled scream of frustration.

When my cell vibrated, I grabbed it, filled with a completely illogical hope that it might be Lanz. It was a text from Tilly:

Tilly: Are you sleeping?

Me: If I was, I wouldn't be texting.

Tilly: :P Are you & Ethan fighting?

Me: No. Why?

Tilly: You 2 had a weird vibe tonight. Andres thinks Ethan's uber-obsessing over invention stuff. Are you suffering from boyfriend neglect?

I fidgeted in my bed. I wanted to talk to her about Lanz, but what if she reacted badly? I thought back to when Ethan and I had first become a couple. Tilly had practically commandeered our relationship, playing matchmaker so that our foursome could stay intact. For the first time ever, I censored what I told my best friend.

Me: No boyfriend neglect. I respect Ethan's focus. Like he respects mine.

Tilly: Ok. What did you think of Lanz and Eve?

I frowned at the screen.

Me: Eve's wrong for him.

Tilly: IDK. Andres saw Lanz kiss her in the parking lot tonight.

My stomach lurched, and I sank back onto the bed.

Me: Kiss kiss?

Tilly: Too dark to tell. But DEFINITELY a kiss.

Tilly: You there?

Tilly: Earth to Mal?

I'd been staring at the screen, dumbfounded. I recovered enough to type a quick note to Tilly.

Me: Here. Sorry. Falling asleep. Talk tmrw?

Tilly: Sure. Nighty-night.

I turned off my phone and lay in the dark, picturing Lanz and Eve kissing. It was better this way, I told myself. Less complicated. I'd stay with Ethan, Lanz would go out with Eve, and all of us would be friends, without anyone's feelings getting hurt. Besides, I had my *Cinderella* audition on Wednesday. Nothing—especially not some crazy unrealistic crush I'd conjured in my mind—was going to distract me.

Chapter Eleven

Waiting in the hall of the conservatory, dressed in my leotard, tights, and pointe shoes, I leaned forward into a deep stretch. With my forehead touching my right knee, I hoped to give off the impression of being focused. But I was hyper-aware of the other dancers in line with me. We were all there to audition for *Cinderella.*

Some girls chatted excitedly, while others' faces were pinched with concentration, or even nausea. I could relate, especially when I saw Violet breezing through the door, smiling and nodding to the other dancers like a queen nodding to her court.

"I have to be someplace by four," she was saying to the girls at the back of the line. "Would you mind if I just . . . ?" Before anyone could complain or even answer, Violet glided to the front of the line, until she stood directly behind me.

"Malie." She nodded hello. "You must be so nervous."

I gave her my best nonchalant smile, then glanced at the glass doors leading to Main Street. I scanned the sidewalk for Ethan. He'd promised he'd be here. Where *was* he?

"I'll come as soon as the list of kids moving on to the National Invention Convention is posted," he'd said. He'd been talking about "the List" since Monday's Invention Convention, when he'd presented his lifesaving surfboard to the judges. I'd snapped the pic of him and Eve holding their ribbons (they'd tied for first place). But no sooner had he taken down his trifold display than he refocused on making it to nationals. I wasn't surprised. This was how it was every year. Only this year, I had this huge chance with the *Cinderella* audition, and I secretly wanted him to make a big deal out of it. My head understood the unspoken deal we had—that both of us would understand each other's focus on our goals. But my heart? These days, my heart didn't know what to feel. It had been in a dizzying pirouette since the carnival. I wasn't the only one noticing, either. So far this week, Tilly had ribbed me at least a dozen times between classes or at lunch.

"Is it the audition?" she'd asked, then added as a side note to Andres, "I told you someday she'd snap under the pressure."

It wasn't only the audition. I couldn't admit to her how often since the carnival I'd caught myself daydreaming about Lanz. How often I'd scanned the hallways for a glimpse of him with Eve. I'd seen them walking together a few times, and my stomach had turned to a block of ice. Lanz still ate lunch with us, and I saw him at Once upon a Scoop, but lately he was quiet and distracted, not at all his chatty, exuberant self.

I glanced out the conservatory door again. No sign of Ethan, and I was next in line to audition. Violet's appearance wasn't doing anything to calm me, either. *Come on*, I told myself, *get it together*.

"Being nervous helps me," I said to her.

Her laugh was a tinkling bell, too practiced to be real. "I used to get nervous, too. Back when I was starting out. If this doesn't work out for you, there'll be so many other chances. Remember that." She smiled sweetly.

"Thanks," I said, vowing not to let her pretenses unhinge me.

"Malie Analu?" A woman was holding the studio door open. "You're up."

After one final glance toward the empty sidewalk, I stepped into the studio. My heart struck walloping beats against my ribs. I took in the five poker-faced judges seated at a long table. Only Signora Benucci gave me the slightest hint of a smile.

"You may begin," the stern-looking man at the end of the table said.

I settled into fourth position. *You're ready*, I reminded myself. I'd broken in my pointe shoes more over the weekend, and even managed to sneak in a couple extra hours of practice in the school gym during lunchtime. My toes and arches still ached, but I could tell they were already stronger than they'd been just the week before.

I pushed off from fourth position, *tombé*-ing with one leg as I swung my supporting leg up, performing a series of step-over turns. Then I moved into a *pas de bourrée*, imagining myself as a bird, perching on a branch, then fluttering up, down, up, down, up. The moves I'd choreographed with Signora Benucci flowed together. That's when I felt it—the magic moment when everything fused and my legs and arms felt like music and motion combined.

As I finished my final pirouette and moved into a low curtsy for the judges, I broke into a smile. No matter what happened, I'd danced my best for them. I felt the truth of it in the tingling of my limbs, in the happiness hurtling through my veins.

I barely saw Violet or the other waiting dancers as I left the studio and changed into my street shoes; adrenaline turned the hallway into a heady blur. When I stepped out into the sunshine and saw no sign of Ethan, my exhilaration dampened. He hadn't come. But as soon as the thought flashed through my mind, a second one came behind it, a voice censuring me. *Who were you really hoping for?* the voice whispered. *Ethan? Or Lanz?*

I struggled to silence the voice. *Of course it was Ethan. It's always been Ethan.* But . . . what if I'd outgrown "always"? What if "always" didn't fit Ethan and me—us—anymore?

I pulled out my phone. Five text messages. Three from Tilly—each one exhibiting more and more frustrated emoji faces—asking for an update on the audition, one from Andres's phone (but really it was Tilly again), and one from Lanz. I read Lanz's last.

Dance well, Malie. Make them believe. Like I do already.

My hand trembled as I stared at the screen, my heart lifted by his words. Then my phone vibrated, making me jump. There it was. A text from Ethan:

So sorry! Lost track of time. I'm sure you did great.
PS I made nationals! We're at Pizza Rita's celebrating.
Come by?

I pictured him hanging out with his Invention Convention buds, toasting their victories over slices of supreme pizza (his favorite). Even after my great audition, I wasn't in the mood for that. But this wasn't anger. It was the gnawing feeling of something shifting inside me, of some of the expectations that I'd had about Ethan and me blurring with confusion and doubt.

Slowly, I texted Ethan back: **Got to get to the Scoop. Call you later.**

It was a simple text, but it felt like the beginning of something immense.

· · · · · · ·

I had just gotten to school the next morning when it happened. As I stood at my locker with Tilly and Andres, my cell vibrated with an email. I knew it would be from the conservatory. I managed a weak "It's here" to Tilly, who promptly made a grab for my phone, which I swept out of her reach.

"Let me see." Tilly jumped up and down.

"Just . . . give me a sec." I leaned against my locker, clutching the phone to my chest. Since yesterday, waiting had been excruciating. Of course, Mom had had no idea why I was so on edge.

"What's gotten into you?" she'd asked last night, when I'd kicked the door of the deep freeze for not opening on the first try. "Is something wrong at school?"

I couldn't tell her, but the guilt of keeping the secret from her only added to my moodiness.

Now I closed my eyes. *I'll be happy with any part,* I told myself. *Any part at all.*

Holding my breath, I opened the email. I had to reread it twice before the words sank in:

Dear Ms. Analu,

It is with great pleasure we offer you the principal role of Cinderella in our June 1 performance. Daily rehearsals will be held 4–6 p.m., Mon–Sat. Attendance is mandatory . . .

"I'm in," I whispered as Tilly and Andres, who'd been reading over my shoulder, whooped and grabbed me in a crushing hug. "I'm in!" I laugh-shrieked.

"Not just in." Tilly squeezed my hands. "You're Cinderella!" She stepped into the middle of the hallway and yelled, "Attention, peeps! My best friend is going to be a famous ballet dancer someday. So you better be picking up your trash, or she'll tell the world that global warming's all your fault." A few kids slowed as they passed her, and she raised a threatening eyebrow at them. "That's right. You heard me." She turned to me. "I need to post this on my blog! We could do a role-model spin on you, talk about your conservation efforts . . ."

I yanked Tilly back toward my locker, giggling. "Famous is a teensy bit premature, Till. But thanks for the love . . ."

My voice died as I saw Violet walking in our direction, her lips in a composed smile.

"Malie." Her arms went around me in a barely there hug. "Congratulations."

"Thanks."

She held me at arm's length, as if she were an adult appraising a child. "I didn't know you had it in you. Cinderella! I can*not* believe it!"

"Me neither." I fidgeted with my schoolbag as an awkward silence settled between us. "So . . . what part did you get?"

"I'll be Fairy Godmother." Her careful smile quivered. "And they've told me I'll be your sub for the part of Cinderella." She waved a hand. "They always have to assign substitutes, because . . . well, you never know, do you?" She glanced down at the floor. "This is the first year I won't be dancing as principal."

"I know. I'm—I hope you're not too disappointed?" I would've been, if I'd been in her position, and that made me feel a twinge of guilt, even through my excitement.

Her lips quivered faster, but she shrugged. "I've had plenty of chances in the spotlight. It's only fair to give somebody else a shot. And anyway, I have a long dancing life ahead of me."

"That's a great way to look at it. It'll be fun to work together. You'll be a terrific Fairy Godmother."

She tilted her head at me. "Aw. That's sweet of you." She gave me one more smile, then said, "I better go. You'll want to spread the news." She gestured to my cell phone. "I'll bet your mom is going to be speechless!"

She breezed down the hallway as my stomach hardened into a boulder of dread.

"My mom." I gave Tilly a pleading look. "How am I going to tell her?"

Tilly rolled her eyes. "Open mouth. Words pour out. Simple. I mean, no school project goes on for this long. I'm surprised she hasn't caught on already."

"We've been so busy at the parlor . . ." I sighed, thinking about all the ways the conversation with Mom could go so wrong. "She won't be happy I lied. Or that rehearsals will take up so much time."

"Mal." Tilly's gaze was stern.

"Okay, okay. I'll tell her. Only . . . not yet. I'll start rehearsals, get a good feel for the routines, and *then* I'll tell her." Suddenly, I wanted desperately to change the subject, and then I had the way to do it. "Ethan!" I blurted out. "I've got to tell Ethan!"

I took off at a jog toward the science lab, leaving Tilly and Andres staring after me.

· · · · · · ·

I was about to burst into the science lab, but I saw something through the door's window that stopped me.

Ethan and Eve were bent over a beaker, deep in conversation about whatever they were witnessing in a frothing blue substance. Ethan grazed Eve's hand with his fingertips. It could've been that he was showing her how to measure some of the powder she was holding, or it could've been flirting. It *definitely* had a flirting look to it, and yet they both seemed innocently oblivious.

I blushed, feeling like a spy. Could I be angry at Ethan for something he didn't realize he was doing? Did I even feel angry? Or was I simply surprised? I hardly knew. I stood frozen for a few seconds more until Greg, another kid in the science club, brushed past me into the room. He dropped his backpack onto a desk with a clang, making Ethan and Eve jump. When they caught sight of me standing in the doorway, they stepped apart instantly.

Eve gave me an embarrassed smile. "Malie! Hey!"

Ethan walked toward me, his face cranberry. "Hey, you." He gave a backward glance to Eve, then mumbled, "We were finishing up an experiment."

I nodded, deciding not to overthink what I'd just seen. I could've imagined it, and besides, Ethan wouldn't ever intentionally do anything to hurt me. And Eve had Lanz now. At least, I *thought* she did. My stomach twisted, but I shook the feeling away. This was a good day. A *great* day. I wasn't about to psychoanalyze it into ruins.

Which was what made me announce "I'm Cinderella!" a little too loudly, causing everyone in the lab to stare. "In the conservatory's ballet," I added, more softly this time. "I just found out!"

"Mal, that's awesome!" Ethan grinned. "I knew you'd get in!" He stepped closer to hug me, but then hesitated awkwardly, as if he was worried about others seeing. When his arms finally wrapped around me, they rested lightly on my shoulders—the most platonic hug he'd ever given me.

"Thanks." I smiled, even though his congratulations felt a little like a letdown. "I have a lot of work to do. The ballet's June first. A month away."

Ethan frowned. "The first? Oh no." He rubbed his forehead. "That's the weekend of the National Invention Convention. In DC."

"Oh." The bubble of happiness inside me wobbled, threatening to pop. "You promised you'd come."

His face was pained. "I had no idea that the national convention would be that weekend, and I . . . I . . ." He glanced at his feet, looking so torn that I reached for his hand.

"You have to go," I said matter-of-factly. This was what we'd always told each other, that we'd never stand in each other's way. "You can't miss the chance."

Relief crossed his face. "Thanks for seeing that. This is huge for me. It's everything, really."

Everything. I paused over that word. If it was everything, then that made me . . . what? A lump of hurt formed at the back of my throat, and my vow to be understanding was forgotten. "You don't have to look so happy about it," I snapped. Then, when I felt Eve's eyes on me, I spun around and hurried into the hallway.

"Mal, wait!" Ethan caught up to me. "What just happened? You said a second ago that I had to go—"

"I know I did!" I blew out a breath. "That's what I'm *supposed* to say. But I thought . . . that you'd be more upset about missing my performance. Why are you so detached? Shouldn't I matter more to you than that?"

"You matter to me. You know that." His gaze was sincere, making my heart crumple.

"I do. But maybe not the way I *should* matter to you." I swallowed. The niggling fears that had been building inside me over the last few weeks burbled to the surface now. "Ethan. Do you ever wonder if we're *too* right for each other? So right that we're, I don't know, missing something?"

His brow furrowed. "What are you saying? That you're not happy with this anymore? With . . . us?"

My face was burning. "I . . . I don't know. I want to think about this—"

"Ethan?" Eve stuck her head around the door. "The bell's about to ring and we've got to clean up."

"Be there in a sec," he said, then refocused on me. "Mal, if you're saying we should break up—"

"How upset would you be if we *did* break up? Honestly?" I held his gaze until he dropped his eyes in silence. "We're friends. We've always been friends. But friendship isn't the same as dating. Maybe . . . maybe we both need to think about that for a while. On our own."

He opened his mouth to argue, then shut it again. His expression was a maelstrom of frustration and confusion, but he didn't look hurt. When he spoke again, it was a quiet, "Then what?"

I offered him a small smile and a shrug. "Then . . . we see where we are. Okay?"

He peered into my eyes for a long minute, then returned my smile with one of his own. "Okay."

I nodded toward the science lab. "Eve needs your help. I'll . . . call you?"

He gave me a final nod, then disappeared through the door. I headed down the hallway, a bittersweet melancholy settling over me. Had I done the right thing? More important, did I have any idea *what* I was doing anymore?

Chapter Twelve

I flung back my comforter and sat up, checking the time. Twelve a.m. I'd been tossing and turning. I should've been dreaming of *grand-jeté*-ing across the stage in *Cinderella* but instead I was wrestling with a building anxiety. It had taken about a nanosecond for Tilly and Andres to find out about the "talk" Ethan and I had had, and my phone had been buzzing with texts from Tilly all night. I hadn't responded to a single one. I wasn't ready to hear her opinions yet.

I slid open my window, hoping an ocean breeze might lighten the humidity in my bedroom. A full moon blazed in the sky, and as I peered past palm trees toward the water, I saw a familiar ethereal glow along the horizon. My spirits lifted. Was that what I thought it was? It was the right time of year for it. I slipped out of bed and changed from my pj's into shorts and a T-shirt. I left a note for Mom so she'd know where I was, then grabbed my cell.

My fingers hesitated over the screen. There was only one person I wanted to share this with. A week ago, even two weeks ago, I wouldn't have thought twice about texting him, but now? Everything was more complicated. Still, I hadn't seen him since I'd gotten the news about *Cinderella* and, well, I missed him. Pushing all thoughts of how distant he'd seemed lately aside, I texted Lanz:

Me: Are you awake?

I held my breath until a text came back a moment later.

Lanz: Texting with eyes closed would be difficult. ☺
Me: Can you meet me at the cove?

Lanz: Adesso????? It's a full moon. Should I be worried about weremaids?

I smiled.

Me: Only if I throw you overboard.
Lanz: Your jokes are improving every day.
Me: Yours aren't. ☺
Lanz: But you still find them charming.

I laughed, relieved to hear him sounding more like himself.

Me: Don't get cocky or I'll take back the invite. And you don't want to miss this.
Lanz: I'll be there. Let me just leave a note for my mother.

• • • • • • •

Ten minutes later, Lanz found me sitting in the sand by my kayak (last year's birthday gift from Dad), two life jackets beside me. His hair was tousled from sleep, and his mischievous smile shone in the moonlight.

"Here I am." He bowed playfully. "At your bidding. What are my orders, *capitano*?"

"Safety first." I tossed him a life jacket. Once we both had the life jackets on, we dragged the kayak toward the water. I tried not to giggle as Lanz struggled to balance himself on the kayak's seat.

"What? Am I not an expert sailor?" He pushed out his chest in mock-pride, and almost tipped over backward into the waves.

I shook my head between laughs, then pushed the kayak over the cresting waves and climbed in to face him. I picked up my paddle, but hesitated before handing him his. "I'm not sure I can trust you with a paddle."

He inspected it. "If I can master the gelato paddle, I can master this one, too. Besides, I could never let anything happen to Cinderella." He winked.

"So you know I got the part." We paddled farther from shore into the gentle swells. He hadn't been at Once upon a Scoop (Mom told me he'd asked for the afternoon off), and I hadn't wanted to text him. It was the sort of great news you only wanted to share face-to-face.

He nodded. "Eve told me. I saw her after school today."

"Oh." So he'd spent his afternoon with Eve instead of at Once upon a Scoop. "You two seem to get along well."

He nodded. "She's very nice."

"And . . ." I swallowed. Suddenly, I was wishing I'd never texted him to meet me here. "You—you like her?"

He shrugged. "Of course I do! What's not to like?"

I turned my gaze to the shore, wondering if I could turn the kayak around. I could tell him I wasn't feeling well, or that I was tired . . . I just didn't want to be here, in this tiny boat, with nowhere to hide my emotions.

"Well." Lanz scanned the water. "I don't see any were-maids." He leaned toward me. "Are you going to let me in on your secret?"

"What?" I startled at the question. What if he already knew? Knew how every time I was around him, he turned my world topsy-turvy?

He laughed. "Malie. Are you going to tell me why we're

out here? Rowing through the ocean in the middle of the night?"

"Oh. Right." *That* was what he'd meant. I turned my attention to the water. "Give me a second." The tide was calm, quieter than usual, and the moonlight glittered on the water. About twenty feet to our left, an ethereal blue light shimmered beneath the surface. "There!" I pointed to the spot, then motioned for him to row in that direction. Within a minute, we were directly above the glowing water.

Below us, thousands of comb jellies glowed greenish blue, floating gracefully in an underwater light show.

"This is incredible!" he whispered.

"It's bioluminescence," I said. "The comb jellies are only here at certain times of the year. Dad used to bring me out to see them before he moved. Last year he gave me the kayak so I could keep up the tradition. The cove's protected by the breakers, so the current's never strong. Otherwise Mom would never let me come out here on my own."

"Thank you for bringing me here," Lanz said, looking at me.

"I wanted to show you this to thank *you*." I kept my eyes on the water to avoid getting lost in his eyes. "*You're* the reason I'm in *Cinderella*."

He shook his head. "I only introduced you to my mother. Everything that happened after that was your doing. Your talent." He smiled, and the flickering lights from the water reflected on his face. "Mammina doesn't believe in favoritism. Not even for my friends."

Friends. That was all we would *ever* be, and I needed to be okay with it. For the sake of self-preservation, for the sake of Ethan. And Eve. For everyone.

Lanz dipped his paddle gently into the water, causing the jellies to ripple around it in unison, creating one fluttering blanket of blue.

"They look like dancers," Lanz said. "In an underwater ballet."

I nodded. "That's exactly what I used to tell Dad. It's like they choreographed their movements."

"Or not." Lanz shrugged. "Maybe they just . . . connect. No

planning, no practice. Impulsive." His expression was serious, his eyes intent on my face.

A tingle ran up my spine. I had to look away, or else, or else . . . "It's so late. Or . . . early, I guess. We should get back to shore."

"*Cosa c'è?* What's wrong?" He cupped his hands over mine. "I can hear it in your voice. Something's upset you."

I shook my head, yanking my hands out from under his. "Stop! Okay? You can't talk to me like that. Or hold my hands like that! You told me you like Eve! Andres saw you kissing her, and, and . . ." I put my head in my hands. "I don't even understand what's going on anymore!"

I waited, my head down, listening to the lapping water while Lanz sat in stunned silence. Then he laughed.

I peeked up. "How can you possibly be laughing right now?" I glared at him. "Stop, or I swear I'll throw you overboard."

Lanz held up his hands. "*Abbi pietà!* Have mercy! I am not laughing at you. Only . . . that you thought me and Eve were . . . that I kissed her in *that* way. Like a girlfriend."

I stared at him. "Didn't you?"

He shook his head. "No! In Italy, we kiss hello and good-bye, cheek to cheek. It's the custom. I was only trying to be polite with Eve."

My pulse thundered in my ears. "But . . . but you never kissed me cheek to cheek like that."

"Because I was too worried you would slap me!"

I giggled. "That's fair. I might've slapped you."

Lanz's laughter faded, softening into seriousness. "Eve is nice. But she's not the girl for me. I think, actually, that her heart belongs to someone else."

"Ethan," I said, then clamped a hand over my mouth in shock. It was the first time I'd said aloud what I'd been wondering since I'd seen them together in the science lab this morning. Or maybe I'd suspected it for even longer, and I hadn't wanted to admit it to myself.

"It is only a guess," Lanz said quietly, watching me. "But . . . this means you've noticed, too? And . . . are you hurt? Angry?"

"I—I'm not. At least, not the way I thought I might be." I sighed. "Ethan and I are . . . we're taking a break to figure things out."

Lanz's eyes saucered. "Was this his idea or yours?"

"Mine."

"Why?" He said it so quietly I barely heard.

I risked meeting his eyes, and saw something new glinting in them. Hope. My heart thrummed, and suddenly, I gave in to every feeling I'd been pushing away. "Because . . . because I can't think straight around you. That's why I didn't want you to work at Once upon a Scoop. I was scared to spend time with you because I . . . I didn't want to fall for you." There. It was out. The weeks of denying the truth were over.

"Did you?" He leaned toward me until I could smell the scent of his skin—tangy lemon, sand, and sun. "Fall for me?"

"You have to know the answer to that," I whispered, blushing furiously. "But . . . I have plans. Everything has a place in my life. School. Ethan. Dance. And this . . . this complicates everything."

He smiled. "So your life doesn't fit into neat little boxes. *Quel che sarà*. What will be, will be." He brushed my hair from my forehead. "Malie, please. Look at me."

My body was a roller coaster of adrenaline as I lifted my eyes to his. I was terrified; I was elated. I was nauseous; I was lighter than air. I dreaded; I hoped.

"I am Ethan's friend. I am . . . your friend. But since I met you, I've . . . wanted to be more than that to you. I've tried to keep a distance from you lately, but . . . it's not working." His eyes were steady, unblinking. "You asked before why I never kissed you cheek to cheek." He cupped my face in his hands. "There is only one kind of kiss I want to give you."

His lips moved toward mine, until they were so close I could feel their warmth. But—

"Lanz, wait." I pulled away so quickly the kayak swayed. "I can't. I don't want to hurt anyone."

He gazed out over the water, then slowly nodded. "You're right. I don't, either."

"I have to think. And talk to Ethan. But I . . . have a lot to deal with right now with rehearsals . . . I need to focus. Then we can see . . ."

I expected him to say he understood, or that he agreed, but

his relaxed demeanor was gone, replaced with a stiff politeness. "We should get back now." He swung his paddle into the water, turning his eyes toward the shore.

"Oh." My insides crumbled. "Okay."

* * * * * * *

Our ride back to the beach was silent, and as soon as we settled the kayak into the sand, Lanz said he was going home.

I was dismayed. This night was ending all wrong. As he began to walk down the beach, I ran to catch up. "Lanz, wait! Are you . . . are you mad at me?"

He shook his head. "No." Then he threw up his hands. "Well. Maybe . . . Yes!" The moonlight shone on his frown. "You talk about plans and complications. But . . . what is so complicated? You are going to be Cinderella. Your dream is real and happening. You should be less worried now. You should relax. Enjoy this."

"I don't need to relax," I said defensively. "I need to rehearse."

"So rehearse. Dance. Perform. I love that you want to do it all. And I want to be there for you, only . . . I'm not sure you want to let me in."

"I do!" I cried. "I told you I do."

"Then what is it?"

I dug my bare feet into the sand. How could I tell him my fear that even the smallest wrinkle could sabotage all I'd worked so hard for? Things with Ethan were always comfortable and convenient. With Lanz, I felt so unbalanced, so dizzy with like. What would that do to my dance? My focus?

I tried again. "I haven't even told Mom about ballet yet. I have no idea how she'll handle it. That's stressful enough, without adding this into the mix."

"This?" Lanz repeated. "Meaning me?" He ran his fingers through his hair. "Mal, you can't lie to your mom anymore. You have to tell her. But that doesn't have anything to do with us. That's between you and her."

"I know. But I don't need anyone else getting in the way right now . . ." My voice died as his eyes widened, and I realized how my words had sounded.

"*I'm* getting in your way."

"I didn't mean it like that."

"Malie, you haven't been honest with your mom, or yourself.

If you're brave enough to dance in front of hundreds of people, you should be brave enough to fight for what you want."

I glared at him, fury rising in my chest. "You're one to talk. You've been working this whole time at Once upon a Scoop without *your* mom knowing. You don't want to deal with telling her the truth, either."

"It's not the same. I don't want to hurt my mother . . ."

"And lying to her doesn't hurt her?" I countered. "That's an excuse. You're being a hypocrite."

He stared at me, then kicked at the sand. "Forget it!" His voice was tired. "I'll make things easier for you. I won't be a distraction anymore. *Addio.*"

He took off at a run down the beach. I stared after him until he disappeared into the darkness.

Chapter Thirteen

"Well?" I asked, scrutinizing Andres's face as he popped the spoonful of lavender ice cream into his mouth. "How is it?"

Andres blanched, making an effort to swallow even as Tilly shot him a warning look. "It's . . . unusual?" he said tentatively.

"Ach!" I yanked the plastic bowl away from him in frustration. "You *hate* it!" I threw the bowl into the parlor's trash can, then sank back into my chair.

We'd been sitting at our table for the last hour, morning sunlight streaming in through the windows. We'd already attempted a lackluster round of Heads Up!, and now, in an attempt to cheer everyone up, I'd dished out some of my freshly churned ice cream.

Bad idea. Our collective mood had gone from gloomy to down-right morose.

Tilly smacked the back of Andres's head. "Couldn't you have pretended to like it, for crying out loud?"

Andres held up his hands. "I can't help it if Malie's ice cream isn't as good as—"

Another smack, followed by Andres's "Ouch!"

"It's fine," I said despondently. "I know it's not as good as Lanz's. We still have a decent amount of his ice creams and gelatos in the deep freeze, but I'm not sure how long they'll last."

"Well, when's he coming back to work?" Andres asked. "Soon, right?" I felt a pang of guilt. Poor Andres. First Ethan had quit our morning "VIP" time, and now Lanz had quit Once upon a Scoop entirely.

"I don't know." My voice hitched with unease. "He told Mom that he had to help build props for his mother." My voice dropped into a whisper. "For *Cinderella*."

"That's what he told me, too," Andres said forlornly. "I don't get it. He loved working here."

I fidgeted in my chair, not able to look at either one of my friends. I hadn't told them about my fight with Lanz, or why, I suspected, he really wasn't coming to the parlor. He'd promised he wasn't going to distract me anymore, and he was keeping his word. He hadn't been to the Scoop once since our fight, and he avoided me completely at school.

"What's with the long faces?" Mom asked as she appeared at our table. "This isn't like you. I haven't heard a single laugh all morning."

"Maybe you should ask Malie." Tilly folded her arms and sat back in her chair, frowning at me.

"What did *I* do?" I cried, but even as I said it, I knew. I'd driven away Ethan and Lanz, and now everything was off kilter.

Mom focused full parental sensors in our direction, her eyes narrowing as she tried to figure out the problem. "Does this have something to do with that school project you two are working on?"

"What project?" I asked absently, then jolted as Tilly kicked me under the table.

"Your *Scarlet Letter* project," Mom said. "I can't believe how many hours you two have put into it after school. These assignments seem so much more involved now than when I was a kid."

"Oh! Right! *That* project. It's fine," I managed, my voice strung too tight. "Should be done in a few more weeks." Tilly was shooting me death rays now.

"A few more weeks!" Mom's eyes widened. "I'm tempted to call your teacher about this. It's taking up so much of your time."

"You're so right," Tilly said. "We should wrap it up, Mal. ASAP."

My pulse raced. What was she doing? I grabbed her hand and stood up, pulling her toward the kitchen. "Tilly, I need some help with the gelato that's chilling . . ." I improvised.

The second the kitchen door swung shut and we were safely beyond Mom's earshot, I hissed, "Thanks for almost throwing me under the bus out there."

"This is getting old, Mal." Tilly gave me a serious look. "Since this weirdness with you and Ethan started, you don't eat lunch with us at school anymore. Whenever he's with us, you avoid us. And you're still expecting me to keep covering for your ballet stuff? Not cool."

"I'm just . . . really focused right now. I've got to get a handle on the choreography for the ballet, and lunch is a great time to practice. That's all."

It was true, at least, that I had been spending lunch practicing in the school's gym. It was empty then, and there was a mirror along one wall so I could correct my form when I needed to. Only that wasn't all. Not even close. And Tilly, with her radar intuition, wasn't buying it.

"Look," she told me. "I don't know what this whole 'time-out' phase with Ethan is about, but you'll work it out. You two are like me and Andres. Meant to last. Don't give him up just because you think you've outgrown him. You *don't* outgrow love at first sight."

"What if it wasn't? Love at first sight, I mean?" I responded, which made her balk.

"What are you talking about?" She gaped. "*Of course* it was!"

"I'm not sure anymore," I said quietly. "Maybe it was just that

I wanted a version of what you and Andres had. I wanted some-one to hold hands with and crush on."

"Wait, do you really mean that?" she asked.

I was about to say more, but then I heard Mom calling my name from outside.

Tilly blew me a grumbly kiss and left to go get Andres so they could hit the beach.

As soon as they were gone, I got ready to help Mom open the parlor. But first, her eyes lasered in on me.

"Okay, Malie," she said matter-of-factly. "Talk to me. You haven't been yourself all week. Are you missing Dad? Is it some-thing with Tilly? Or Ethan?"

"I'm fine, Mom." *Just keep repeating it until she believes you.*

She restocked the display freezer with a tub of vanilla gelato. "Sometimes I wonder if it might have been . . . easier on you, if we'd moved back to Hawaii when your dad did."

"What?" I gasped. Never, in the three years since the divorce, had she said that before.

"You would see your dad more, and Tutu. Maybe you wouldn't

have gotten so focused on dance. It wouldn't have been your only way of coping."

"I never used dance to cope," I countered.

"I know you think I can never understand how much you loved dance, but ..." She smiled sadly. "Malie, parents have dreams, too. Things they hoped for in their lives. Some of mine came true. Especially in you. Other dreams ... Me and your dad. What I wanted for all of us together as a family ... It didn't work out the way I planned." She pressed her hand against my cheek. "But have I messed up too badly with us? You and me? Have I put too much responsibility on your shoulders? With the parlor, and—"

"Mom, no." I hugged her. "I'm happy here. And the parlor's doing so well now—"

"It's doing well, but who knows for how long? Mr. Sneeves is fickle, and everyone's replaceable." She turned from the freezer to focus her full attention on me. "*That's* why I never wanted dance to become too important to you. When you love something that much, and make it your whole existence, you're bound to be disappointed by it. Someone else will come along who dances better, or you'll get an injury, and then what? Then you have nothing to fall back on."

"So . . . it's better not to take the risk at all? I'll never believe that, Mom. I'm going to start a batch of ice cream," I added quietly before escaping to the kitchen.

I collapsed onto a stool by the ice cream maker just as my phone buzzed with a text from Ethan.

Can we talk? it read. **I know you've been avoiding me. Monday?**

I stared at the text. First Tilly, then Mom, now Ethan. Why did everyone seem to want to talk these days, when that was the last thing I wanted to do? Still, Ethan was right. We *did* need to talk, and it wasn't fair for me to put it off any longer.

Heart hammering in my throat, I replied to his text, telling him I'd meet him in front of the conservatory after school. Then I slipped on my apron and fairy wings, and got to work.

• • • • • • •

I spotted Ethan from a block away, standing outside the conservatory, scribbling in his notebook. Nostalgia flooded me. Ethan's hair was mussed, and his shirt hung crookedly because he'd mismatched the buttons. How was I going to tell him what I knew I had to? How could I cause someone I cared about that kind of hurt?

He glanced up and our eyes met. "Hey, you," he said, like he always did. But today, his voice was constricted, his face flushed. He motioned to a sidewalk bench. "Um . . . should we sit?"

"Sure."

We sat down with a foot of space between us, and neither of us made a move to close the gap.

"I wanted to—" The words came out in unison from both our mouths. We stopped, laughing awkwardly, and a sadness pricked my heart. It was like we were suddenly strangers.

"I'll go first, if that's okay," Ethan said, and I nodded gratefully. He clasped and unclasped his hands in his lap, then straightened. "I've been thinking about how, well, weird things have gotten between us lately. At first I blamed you. I told myself it was because you were so focused on your dancing." I opened my mouth to protest, but he held up his hand. "I know it wasn't you. You weren't doing anything different than you've always done. I wasn't, either. But things changed."

"Or . . . maybe we changed?" I offered.

"Yeah. Maybe." He nodded with relief.

I leaned my head against his shoulder for a second. "Being around you was always so easy. I never wondered why there wasn't more of a—"

"Spark?" Ethan finished for me. "I didn't even realize it was missing until . . ." His voice trailed off and his cheeks flushed darker.

"Eve?" I lifted my head to glance at him as his eyes widened. "It's okay. I thought there might be something between you two."

"There's not! At least, not yet."

"But you want there to be?"

He hesitated, looking pained with guilt. "I don't want to hurt you," he whispered. "But I can't stop thinking about her."

He looked frustrated and lit-up all at once, and I couldn't help laughing. "I get it." It was exactly how I'd been feeling about Lanz. "And I'm not mad, or upset even. You and Eve seem great together. And she's completely in like with you."

His blush deepened. "You think so?"

I nudged him. "There's only one way to find out for sure. Ask her."

"But, Mal, what about you?"

"Don't worry about me. I'm actually relieved. I knew it was time to end things . . ." I sucked in a breath. "But I didn't want to hurt you, either. I'm fine. More than fine." I smiled at him to prove it.

We sat for a few minutes in amicable silence, watching passersby, lost in our thoughts and memories. "You know," Ethan said, "I thought you were starting to like somebody else, too." He studied my face. "You and Lanz? Am I right?"

It was my turn to blush. "Maybe, but . . ." I swallowed. "We got into a fight, and now we're not talking to each other." My voice wobbled, and Ethan gave my hand a brief squeeze.

"Want to tell me about it?"

He said it so openly that seconds later, I was spilling the whole story, as if I was talking to a best friend, which, I realized I *was*. As I finished, Ethan's cell rang, and I saw Eve's name on the screen.

"Take it." I shouldered my schoolbag. "I've got to get to rehearsal anyway."

"I'll call her right back."

We stood up, both of us seeming unsure of how to bring our talk to an end. Then, because I didn't want to regret *not* doing it later on, I threw my arms around him in a hug. "Thank you," I whispered. "For being a great boyfriend. And for being my first kiss."

His arms tightened around me. "We'll stay friends."

I nodded, even though I knew there'd be a while when we kept our distance, not out of any hard feelings, but to let each other breathe and figure things out. We'd come back to the friendship eventually.

I pulled away, turning toward the conservatory's door. "See you at school."

Ethan headed down the sidewalk, already refocused on his phone, probably dialing Eve's number. Then, just as I was about to step inside, he called my name, making me stop.

"Don't give up on Lanz," he said, making me blush all over again. "He's into you."

I wanted to believe him. But I didn't know what to think.

Two hours later, I walked out of the conservatory, dripping with sweat. Rehearsal tonight had been grueling, and Signora Benucci had been especially unrelenting, demanding that I practice the *grand jeté* portion of the final dance over and over again, until my legs were shaking from the effort. I was performing several dances with my *pas de deux* partner, Will, and coordinating our timing and movements proved challenging, even though it was exciting, too. Will had already mastered each of our lifts, but my extensions and form still needed honing.

"You must stretch yourself," Signora Benucci told me. "It's not simply a jump. You are taking flight."

It was hard to take flight with Violet glaring at me from the corner of the room, whispering to her friends. She wasn't happy about me being cast as Cinderella, but with each passing rehearsal, I kept hoping she'd get over it. So far, that hadn't happened, and her hard stares were taking their toll on my dancing.

As I walked down the street, my earbuds in, I was so preoccupied that I nearly slammed into Tilly.

"Malie," she told me, arms crossed. "We have to talk!"

"Tilly," I breathed in exasperation, and removed my earbuds. "I'm guessing you know that Ethan and I broke up."

She tapped one foot against the concrete. "You bet your leotard I do. What are you *doing*?"

"It wasn't just me who made the decision." I started walking in the direction of the parlor, and she followed. "Ethan wanted it, too. We've been heading that way for a while." I gave her a sideways glance. "Don't tell me you haven't noticed. He's fallen for Eve, and I'm—I'm—"

"Well, he can *unfall* for her," she countered. "What about our foursome? It doesn't work without you two."

I stopped, taking in her creased forehead, her downcast eyes. "It's not like we're not going to hang out with you and Andres anymore. It'll just be . . . different."

She shook her head. "You should've left it alone. Things could stay the way they are."

I stiffened. "You and Andres have each other, and you're happy. Ethan and I have to find our ways, too. If Eve comes on board, we'll be a fivesome, and if—if I find somebody else, then—"

"Lanz," Tilly blurted. "You mean Lanz, right?"

"Lanz and I aren't even talking right now!" I threw up my hands. "But you should be happy for me, no matter who I end up with. Or if I end up with nobody at all!"

"Maybe I would be, if you would actually talk to me, instead of keeping everything to yourself! You don't say boo for weeks on end, and now I have to find out from Andres that my two best friends are breaking up." She glared at me. "I always thought you could tell me anything."

I stared at her, floored by the hurt in her face. "I—I'm sorry. But I didn't know what I felt for the longest time. Or how to talk about it."

"You could've tried me."

"Tilly, come on. You know what you would've said."

Tilly nodded. "What I'm *still* going to say! That you and Ethan belong together."

I sighed. "You're saying that because you don't want anything to change."

"Of course I don't!"

I rubbed my temples. "What about what I want? What's

right for me? I'm so sick of everyone telling me what I can and can't do!" I yelled these words loud enough that some people passing by on the sidewalk moved to give me a wider berth. "This is why I didn't tell you before," I added, trying to speak more quietly. "Because I was afraid of *this* happening. I—I can't deal right now." My voice broke, and I turned away.

If she called my name, I didn't hear it. All I heard was Tchaikovsky booming through my earbuds, drowning out every other sound but my hammering, hurting heart.

Chapter Fourteen

The moment I walked into Once upon a Scoop, I knew something was terribly wrong. Mom's face—pale and angry—was enough to tell me.

She knew. She knew everything.

I glanced at the line of customers, hoping that she'd have to deal with them instead of me. No such luck.

"Ladies and gentlemen." Her voice, on the surface, seemed calm enough, but I could hear the current of fury underneath. "The shop will be closed to customers for the next ten minutes. My sincerest apologies and gratitude for your patience." She ushered them out the door, issuing coupons for free ice cream cones. "We'll reopen as quickly as we can."

My skin turned clammy as she flipped the sign on the door to CLOSED. Then she faced me, her eyes full of disappointment. She let loose a string of Hawaiian—something she only did when she was absolutely beside herself.

"How could you?" she said, switching to English. "All these weeks I believed you were going to Tilly's. Doing school-work. And—and now I learn that you've been dancing? Behind my back?"

"I was *going* to tell you," I started helplessly.

"Instead I find out from this Violet girl I've never met!" She put her head in her hands.

So it had been Violet who'd told Mom. I shouldn't have been shocked, especially with Violet peeved over losing the Cinderella part. Now I had no defense, no excuses. Not that it mattered. I was wrong to lie, and now I was going to pay the price.

"It was humiliating," Mom continued. "She came into the shop to congratulate me, she said, on your great accomplish-ment. 'What accomplishment?' I ask. And she says, 'Don't you know?' And then she tells me about *Cinderella*." Her eyes bored into me, stabbing my chest with regret. "I have to hear all of it from a stranger! Because my own daughter has been lying to me!"

"Violet shouldn't have told you. It wasn't any of her business—"

"*You* had no business disobeying me!" Mom cried. "Violet can't be blamed for your poor judgment."

Suddenly, the frustrations of the day, of the past weeks, exploded from my mouth in a torrent of words. "What was I supposed to do? You told me I couldn't dance anymore. I tried to talk to you about it, but you wouldn't listen! You didn't care how much it hurt me to give it up! All you care about is this parlor with its lame ice cream!"

Mom held up a warning finger to my face. "The source of our livelihood is *not* lame. We couldn't live here without this shop and the income it gives us—"

"I know that! But it will never be what I want." My chest was burning, my eyes welling. "My dancing at the conservatory wasn't costing us anything! Signora Benucci was teaching me for free.

And you had Lanz here to help! You weren't stressed about the business anymore. I arranged everything, and I thought—"

"You thought only of yourself." Mom's voice was thick with distress. "You disrespected me by disobeying."

"I've tried so many times to get you to understand, but you never will." I leaned toward her, reaching for her hands. She pulled them away. "Makuahine, I'm so sorry I lied to you. I was wrong. Please, let me show you what I can do. Come watch me at rehearsal. See how far I've come. I'm on pointe now. I'm the principal ballerina—"

"Not anymore you're not." The words, thorny and brutal, wedged in my heart. "The conservatory will find a replacement for you."

I froze, stunned. "No." It came out quietly but firmly. "You can't take it away from me."

"I can," she said simply. "I will."

My eyes filled with tears. "Why would you do that to me?"

She turned toward the kitchen. "Because you put dancing above all else, even your family. Reality is responsibility and work and school. Reality is *not* following a fantasy that can never last. It is not hurting your family with dishonesty."

My tears spilled over my cheeks. "Don't do this—"

"Malie. It is done." She paused in the doorway to the kitchen to glance back at me. "Open the shop now, please."

Then she disappeared into the kitchen, leaving me with my tears, and customers peering through the shop's front window, waiting for their ice cream. I sucked in a shaky breath and opened the door, as my dream of being Cinderella melted away.

• • • • • • •

"Malie?" Ethan touched my shoulder and I jumped, dropping my binder on the floor.

"Oh!" was all I could manage as I slipped my earbuds from my ears, remembering where I was. It was Monday, exactly one week since Mom had banned me from dance. I was at school. Standing in the hallway at my locker. That's right. At least, I was *physically* at school. Mentally, I was in a colorless, mind-numbing world without dance. "Sorry," I said. "I didn't see you before."

Ethan peered at me with concern, and I noticed Eve

standing beside him. In some distant corner of my mind, I registered that they were holding hands. "I—we—wanted to make sure you were okay." Ethan glanced at Eve. "We heard about what happened with your mom and *Cinderella*. It's lousy."

"Let me guess. Violet told you?" She'd wasted no time telling the entire student body that she'd reclaimed the Cinderella role for herself.

"Actually, Lanz told us."

"Oh." Another pain shot through my heart. So he knew, but he still wouldn't talk to me.

"How are you? Really." Ethan's voice was so full of compassion that I nearly started crying right then and there. What could I say? I was breathing. I was eating. Sleeping. Going to school. I was scooping ice cream every day, wearing a plastered-on smile. I was existing. But each day that passed without dance dragged slower than an *adagio battement fondu*. There was a void inside me that nothing could fill.

"I'm surviving." I strove to give my voice some brightness. "Mom pretty much grounded me for life."

"What about your dad?" Ethan asked. "He understood, right?"

I shook my head. "He pulled the 'united front' card on me and backed Mom."

I remembered what he'd said to me when I'd FaceTimed with him, hoping for sympathy. "Your punishment isn't about you dancing or not dancing," he'd said. "This is about you breaking our trust."

It brought a fresh scarlet shame to my cheeks, just thinking about it.

"Maybe Lanz's mom could do something?" Eve suggested kindly. "Talk to your mom, maybe?"

"No."

Each afternoon, I walked home from school past the conservatory to watch the rehearsals through the window. Signora Benucci always paused in her instruction to nod at me through the glass, her expression mirroring my own—disappointed, helpless. Telling her that I wouldn't be dancing was one of the toughest things I'd ever had to do. I admired her so much, and I was failing her. But she'd told me she wouldn't get involved in a family matter like this.

"You have such talent," she'd said. "It's a waste to let it slip away."

Her words were what I'd always dreamed of hearing, but knowing that they'd stay words, that they'd never translate into performances, or a chance at joining a dance company—that made them salt in an open wound.

"There's nothing anyone can do," I said to Ethan and Eve now. "But . . . I'm still dancing."

Ethan gave me a questioning look. "What? How?"

"During lunch in the gym." It wasn't even close to the same as the conservatory, but I didn't care. It was all I had. "I need to."

Ethan nodded in understanding. "I know."

I swallowed thickly, wanting to be done with this topic. But, since I was already in the throes of torment, I decided to ask the question that had been gnawing at me since Ethan had mentioned his name. "How's Lanz doing?" I didn't even try for subtlety. There wasn't any point, and I was too out of sorts to fake anything right now anyway. "I haven't seen him around school lately."

"Um," Ethan and Eve said in unison, and the distress on both their faces made my pulse skip with dread.

"What?" I whispered.

Ethan sucked in a breath, then blurted, "He left town."

I'd been fidgeting with my books and schoolbag, trying to make it through the conversation without my eyes filling, but now there was no stopping the tears. "What do you mean 'left town'?"

"He went back to Italy." Ethan and Eve exchanged another worried glance. They were so in sync with each other, they already seemed natural as a couple. "Last Thursday. I—I figured he told you?"

"No." The air left my lungs. "I haven't had my cell." Mom had taken it away when she'd grounded me. "We—we haven't talked since our fight. Why did he go back?" *And for how long?* I wanted to ask. *Forever?* The thought made me cold all over.

Ethan shrugged. "He didn't say. But . . ." He pulled a small box out of his backpack. "He asked me to give you this. Sorry it took me a few days to get it to you. I . . ." He looked sheepish. "Forgot to pick it up from the conservatory."

I nearly smiled. That was so Ethan-ish of him to forget.

He set the box in my palm and my fingers instinctively closed around it, as if hoping it might still hold some warmth from when Lanz had held it. "Thanks." I suddenly wanted to be alone, with the box, with my thoughts. "Um . . ."

"We should get going, Ethan." Eve offered me an empathetic smile.

I returned it gratefully, glad that she understood what I needed at that moment.

She waved and started down the hallway, but Ethan stayed behind, motioning to her that he'd be right there.

I mustered up a smile for him, to let him know I was okay with him and Eve being together. "It's working out with you two?" I asked.

He grinned and nodded, then grew serious again. "And Mal, this thing with you and Tilly. She likes Eve; she's just pulling her 'don't rock the boat' routine. She'll come around. You'll see."

"She hasn't said a word to me all week." I sighed. "Seems like everybody's mad at me right now."

"Not everybody. And whatever happened with Lanz, I'm sorry."

I bit my lip to keep it from trembling. "Thanks. Me too."

I watched him and Eve walk down the hallway together, falling into a matching stride. Well, at least one good thing had come out of the colossal mess I'd made: Ethan was happy. And what he'd said about Tilly had given me a small measure of hope.

But what about Lanz? Why hadn't he told me he was leaving? Maybe he'd tried my cell before he left, but I had no way of knowing.

And the worst thought of all: What if he wasn't coming back?

With shaky fingers, I opened the box in my hand. Every doubt I'd had about my feelings for Lanz, every ounce of anger I'd felt toward him since the night on the beach, rushed out of me in a trembling breath.

Nestled in the box was a thin silver necklace with a delicate glass ballet slipper charm. A note was tucked behind the necklace. I unfolded it and read:

Malie,

This is for you. It's my apology, and my wish for you. I'm sorry we fought. You were right about so many things. Mama knows about me working at Once Upon a Scoop now. I told her everything. I was wrong to keep it from her for so long. It's time you and I were honest about what we want. This is why I'm going to be with my father. Mama says it will be good for all of us.

My heart hit the floor. The boy who'd made me fall for him despite every logical reason I had not to . . . was gone for good. And I'd pushed him away, told him I couldn't make time for him and ballet. Why? Because I was scared of losing ballet? Scared I couldn't balance everything in my life that I loved? What an idiot I'd been. I collapsed against my locker, not wanting to finish the note but knowing I had to.

Now my wish for you is that you wear this necklace when you dance on June 1. I know that your mom has said no, but don't give up.

I stared at the note until the five-minute warning bell rang, and I was forced to grab my books for class. Then I tucked the necklace away. It was beautiful, but I didn't want the painful reminder of what I'd lost. First Cinderella, and now Lanz. He was thousands of miles away, and I was stuck here, hanging on to thousands of things I wanted—needed—to say to him.

* * * * * * *

"One scoop or two?" I asked. I watched as the customer struggled to rein in her tantruming toddler.

"What? Oh ... two. With extra crushed pineapple." No sooner had the words left her mouth than her little boy knocked two containers from the counter onto the floor, spraying fruit preserves and M&Ms in every direction. "Liam! Naughty!" She gave me a helpless shrug. "I'm so sorry. He missed his naptime today ..."

Outwardly, I managed a monotone, "Don't worry. I'll clean it up." Inwardly, I screamed. If Lanz had been here, he would've turned this moment into fun with some good-natured jokes or an entertaining clean-up dance routine. He would've had everyone in the shop laughing, including me. There was no laughter this afternoon.

I checked my watch. It was only four o'clock. Another four hours to go till closing time, and right now I was manning the shop solo, while Mom went over the month's profits with Mr. Sneeves in the back office.

I had nearly finished sweeping up the last of the mess when a familiar voice made my stomach turn to sludge.

"Wait until you see my tutu," Violet gushed as she stepped through the door along with a group of her friends. "All the costumes were donated from the American Ballet Theatre. They performed *Cinderella* last season. I'm telling you, it's gorgeous!"

I focused my attention on the floor, but then I heard, "Oh, Malie!" followed by Violet's tinkling laugh. "I almost didn't see you down there."

I stood up, gritting my teeth. "What can I get for you today?"

Violet slid into a chair by the window and her friends followed suit. "The works! Four Fairy-Tale Ambrosia sundaes and four banana splits. You'll bring them to the table, right?"

I nodded through my irritation. Violet *would* show up on one of the worst days ever. I scrambled to make the sundaes, hoping that the faster I made them, the faster she and her friends would leave. Already my eyes burned from holding back tears. Right when I couldn't bear another word, Violet walked toward me.

"Malie." Her voice was quiet, dripping with faux sympathy. "I'm sorry about what happened with this *Cinderella* mix-up. I was positive you'd already told your mom about getting the part, otherwise I never would've said anything." She offered me a peacemaking smile. "I hope you're okay, and that there are no hard feelings."

At first, I couldn't even speak. How dare she feign regret? My throat closed in anger, my body turning rigid with the effort of staying calm. Finally, I uttered a strangled, "It's fine. I'm fine. No worries."

Violet golf clapped, and for a moment seemed to contemplate hugging me. The fierce look in my eyes made her think better of it. "What a relief," she said as she glided back to her table. "I knew you'd understand."

I blinked rapidly, refusing to give Violet the satisfaction of seeing tears. Then I refocused on the two trays of sundaes and splits before me, adding sprinkles and hot fudge. Meanwhile, Violet unveiled the Cinderella costume from a garment bag. It was a breathtaking shade—pearlish pink like the inside of a conch shell. It was covered in iridescent sequins, with a delicate heart-shaped neckline.

"It has to be taken in," Violet was saying over her friends' oohs and aahs. "But look at this. Sixty layers of tulle in the tutu! It's the real deal."

My breath came quick as I slid my hands under the trays. Balancing them precariously, I started for Violet's table. *Just get through it*, I told myself.

I didn't see the puddle of strawberry preserves in my path until my right heel skidded through the slick. A second later I was sitting on the floor, stunned, as trays and sundae bowls clattered down around me.

"Oh my god," shrieked Violet, staring down at her costume in horror. "Look what you did!"

Ignoring the preserves and chocolate sauce dripping from my own hair, I stood up and stared at the red and brown splatters across the bodice of the Cinderella costume. "I'm so sorry." My voice quivered. "Let me soak it in some cold water—"

"Are you kidding?" Violet's face was the color of the strawberry preserves, her mouth curled into a scowl. "You did this on purpose, just to ruin it for me!"

"I didn't!" I cried. " I slipped—"

"What on earth?" Mom's voice came from behind me, and I turned to find her staring at the scene in horror, Mr. Sneeves right behind her.

I opened my mouth to explain, but before I could, Violet exploded, "This is the worst customer service I've ever received." She jabbed a finger in my direction. "She deliberately spoiled this costume, and her attitude is completely unacceptable."

Mr. Sneeves stepped forward. "My deepest apologies. If you'd allow me, I'd be happy to have the costume dry-cleaned—"

Violet pulled the costume protectively to her chest. "No one in this shop touches this costume." She stared at me. "I never would've expected you to be so cruel, Malie." With that, she barreled out of the shop, her friends in her wake.

"Miss Analu." Mr. Sneeves's voice was deadly calm. "A word in the kitchen. Now."

I could barely look at Mom as we followed Mr. Sneeves into the kitchen.

"Mr. Sneeves," I began as the kitchen door swung shut, "this was a terrible accident—"

"No. I don't think so." He scowled as he turned to Mom. "Your complete inability to exert control over your daughter's behavior has led to a level of unprofessionalism I never should've ignored."

Mom shook her head, an apology already forming on her lips.

"Unprofessionalism?" I repeated before Mom had the chance to speak. The fury building in my throat poured out of me. "I'll tell you what's unprofessional, Mr. Sneeves. You criticize my mother for the way she runs this parlor, even though she works extra hours *without overtime pay* to make sure it's successful. She deserves your respect, and if you would pull your head—"

"Malie!" Mom grabbed my arm, pressing it firmly. "Enough."

"No, Mom. I can't stand it—"

"Go home." Her eyes were commanding, unflinching. "Now."

I glared at Mr. Sneeves, whose face had gone from white to purple with rage, and suddenly a panicky doom washed over me. What had I done?

"No." Mr. Sneeves's tone was an ominous bell tolling. "*Both* of you go home." He stared at Mom. "You're finished here. Permanently."

The tears I'd been holding back for hours now—tears of regret over Lanz, of fury toward Violet, of injustice for Mom—overflowed.

I turned, and without another word, without waiting for Mom, without even looking at her, which I knew would break my heart, I left the shop. Forever.

Chapter Fifteen

I smiled, listening to the sound I loved—the soft thud of ballet shoes landing on wood—as I leapt across the stage, basking in the spotlight. Then the thudding grew louder, more urgent.

I opened my eyes, then instantly wished I hadn't. The reality of the last twenty-four hours crushed the remnants of my dream. I sat up in bed. The thudding—no, it was tapping—turned manic.

I looked out the window. Tilly was glaring at me from the second-floor landing, motioning for me to come outside.

I glanced at the clock. Seven a.m. *Aue!* I'd overslept, and school started in half an hour! I leapt out of bed and cranked open my window. As soon as I did, Tilly stuck her head inside.

"What do you think, it's summer vacation? Get up already."

I temporarily pushed aside my shock that Tilly was speaking to me after days of the cold shoulder. I pulled my hair into a mussed knot and threw on some clothes. "I can't believe how late it is," I said, dashing into the bathroom to brush my teeth. "Mom never lets me oversleep."

"I don't think she's here," Tilly said. "I knocked on the front door first." When I came back into the room, she added, "I've been standing out here for ten minutes trying to wake your sorry butt up. The lengths I go to for you."

I paused mid–shoe tying. "Is that a Tilly-style apology?" I desperately hoped it was, because I especially needed my best friend after the Once upon a Scoop debacle yesterday. Even now, fresh tears threatened.

"Waterworks already?" Tilly said. "I didn't even say sorry yet."

"I know," I blubbered. "But . . . I've missed you. And my life is a calamity."

Tilly climbed through the window and swiftly grabbed me in a hug. "I doubt it. If I hadn't noticed the sea turtle caught in the fishing net on my walk here. Or rescued it. Or told off the surfer that was ignoring it on the beach. *That* would've been a calamity. But . . . try me. I'll be the judge."

Five minutes later, I'd told her everything—Lanz leaving, the fiasco with Violet, Mom getting fired.

"Whoa," she said. "That qualifies. For sure."

I nodded morosely. "And I can't undo any of it."

"Nope. It's like one of your sundaes. Once it melts, there's no saving it. Unless you like ice cream soup." She shrugged when I gave her a doubtful look. "Hey, *I've* always been a fan." I giggled, and she smiled triumphantly. "Laughter. A good sign."

I shook my head. "What am I going to do?"

She squeezed my shoulder. "Go to school, first off. Second . . . email Lanz to tell him how you feel."

"What good will it do now?"

She stuck her hands on her hips. "Look at all the trouble lying's cost you. Telling him the truth certainly can't make things worse." She handed me her cell. "Get your brave on. Do it now. Andres got his email address before he left."

I looked askance at her. "You never even wanted Lanz and me to get together."

"Hey. I needed time to process." She jabbed a finger at her phone, dictated Lanz's email address to me, then disappeared into the bathroom to give me some privacy.

I logged into my email and wrote:

```
Dear Lanz,

Thank you for the necklace. It's beautiful.
There are so many things I want to say to you,
but email doesn't seem like the right place to
do it. I wish we could talk face-to-face, only
now you're gone. So here goes . . . I'm sorry,
too. I never meant to make you feel like you
weren't important to me. You ARE. I wish I could
show you how much. I wish you'd come back.
Because . . . you've melted my heart.

Love,

Malie
```

My hand hesitated, but I closed my eyes and hit SEND before I lost my nerve.

Tilly stuck her head around the bathroom door. "Did you tell him that you'll travel to the ends of the earth to be with him and his gelato?"

I tossed a pillow at her, but then she checked the time and whistled. "Come on or we'll be late."

I grabbed a yogurt and banana from the fridge, read the note Mom had left on the table saying she had an early appointment in town, and left for school with Tilly. It was such a relief to be hanging out with her again that I felt the tiniest bit better.

"By the way, I *am* sorry." Tilly kicked at an orphaned seashell, keeping her eyes fixed on it as it tumbled down the sidewalk. "I know I overreacted to your breakup with Ethan."

"It wasn't just *my* breakup," I said quietly. "Ethan wanted it, too."

Tilly nodded. "I had this idea in my head of how things would be. How they *should* be."

"I know. But our friendship's too important to let any boy get in the way of it. Ethan or Lanz or . . . whoever. We can be there for each other through the changes, right?"

"I hate change," Tilly grumbled, kicking the shell into a nearby oleander bush.

I smiled. "You can't hate change. Since you were ten you've been swearing you're going to change the world by stopping global warming."

She laughed. "That's true."

We walked for a few minutes in comfortable silence, but when we rounded the corner to school, I froze. Violet stood on the school steps, talking to her friends. The frown on her face said it all.

"Guess who she's badmouthing?" I moaned. "I changed my mind. I can't do school today."

"Yes. You can." Tilly steered me back toward the doors. "Your mom lost her job, your crush left the country, and you're freaking out over *her*?" She scoffed. "Perspective, Mal."

I climbed the steps to face Violet's cutting glare. "Hi, Violet," I tried. Her glare darkened. "I just want to say I'm sorry. Again. For your costume. And . . . I'll pay for a new one." I had no idea how I'd be able to afford it, but that didn't matter.

Violet waved away the offer. "Mr. Sneeves had it dry-cleaned overnight," she said, then added a reluctant, "he dropped it off at our house this morning. It's fine, thank god. I mean, a costume from the ABT? You can't just *buy* a new one at the mall."

I bit back the angry remarks I was tempted to say. "I'm glad."

Her rigid expression softened a smidge. "I heard your mom got fired. That stinks." I blinked in surprise at the sincerity in her tone. "Was it because of what happened yesterday?"

I hesitated, tempted to make her feel responsible, but I was done with lying. "It happened for a lot of reasons," I finally said.

"Oh." Her obvious relief annoyed me. I imagined her thinking, *Not my problem. Phew.*

"Well . . . good luck with *Cinderella*," I said hastily, wanting to finish this convo before it took a turn for the worse. "You'll be great."

"Thanks." Violet nodded, not smiling, but seeming to respect me for saying it.

I waved, then made a beeline for the doors with Tilly beside me.

"At least that's over with," Tilly said.

"Yeah, but I don't feel any better," I said glumly.

She squeezed my hand. "You'll get there."

I sighed. It would take an eternity.

• • • • • • •

I lifted into a *relevé*, then lowered my feet, frowning. I'd been running through the *Cinderella* routines in the school gym for the last half hour, even though I was certain I'd never perform them for anyone but myself. It didn't matter. I couldn't stop. Except today, my pointe shoes were telling me something different.

I sat down to examine the shoes, pressing my fingers against the tips. Sure enough, the toe boxes were nearly worn through. My pointe shoes were dead.

It wasn't surprising. This was the pair that Signora Benucci had given me. I'd been trying to make them last, but with all my practicing, they'd worn out faster. Who knew when—or if—I'd ever have another pair?

I leaned back against the gym's mirror, closing my eyes. Instantly, I saw myself under the spotlight, dressed in that pearly pink costume, pirouetting across the stage. I dropped my head to my knees, trying to shake the image from my mind. I couldn't keep doing this to myself. Violet was Cinderella now.

I slipped off my pointe shoes, cradling them in my palms for a long minute, blinking back tears, feeling like I was about to say good-bye to a best friend.

"Don't cry," a voice whispered in my ear, and then familiar, oh-so-welcome arms went around me. "*Ku'u momi makamae*, my precious pearl, it's going to be okay."

"Mom?" I managed through my tears. She hadn't called me a pearl since I was a preschooler. It had been her and Dad's pet name for me, and now it only made me cry harder. "Wh-what are you doing here?"

Mom kissed my forehead and tucked my hair behind my ears. Then she clicked her tongue at my tears, brushing them away with her palm. "No mother ever wants to be the reason for her child's tears." Her voice wavered as she glanced down at my pointe shoes. "I stayed up all night, thinking about you and your dancing." She ran a finger along the toe box of one of the shoes. "I worry that I've been doing all the talking . . . and none of the listening."

"I got you fired," I cried. "I lied to you. I should never have gone behind your back—"

"No," she conceded, "and I won't excuse the lying. But . . . do you know what I spent last night doing?"

I shook my head.

"Watching every one of your ballet recitals. I began to wonder when I turned into someone who's afraid to let her daughter dream. I didn't used to be that way. But when hurt is too deep, it steals courage." Her gaze was far off, and I wondered if she was remembering parts of our life before the divorce. "I've been trying to protect you from that same hurt."

"Taking away dance doesn't protect me. It hurts me." I squeezed her hand. "This is what I've been trying to tell you. Even if I never had a single moment in the spotlight, I'd still love dance. I can't *not* love it. It's part of who I am."

"I see that now." She straightened with resolve. "Which is why it's time I remembered my bravery. For me and for you. So I got up this morning and walked straight to the conservatory. I waited two hours for Signora Benucci to open the studio. Do you know I never realized how much I have in common with her? We talked for an hour!" She smiled. "In fact, we're thinking of doing a girls' night, dinner or coffee. Maybe we can try to get a better handle on this single-parenting thing."

I smiled through my tears. "I don't know, Mom. You're doing okay in the parenting department."

She shook her head. "I can do better. *That's* why I met with Signora Benucci. You see, I had to speak with her, to hear it from her lips."

I felt the smallest hint of hope. "Hear what?"

"What I knew in my heart when I watched the videos. That you have a gift. Rare and worth cultivating. Maybe it wouldn't be my worst mistake as a mother, but it would be the one that would haunt me the most, if I kept you from dance."

"But . . . what are you saying?"

She smiled. "I'm saying that the role of Cinderella belongs to you, if you still want it. Signora Benucci will consider letting you back into the show, if you can prove to her that you're ready."

"I am!" I practically shouted it, and Mom laughed. "I've been rehearsing every day during lunch. I know all the steps—"

Mom held up her hands. "Don't tell me. Tell *her*. At rehearsal tonight. Signora Benucci had an errand to run this afternoon, so it will be later than usual. From six to nine. She says you have a lot of work to do. The performance is only three weeks away, and as much as she wants you to dance, she's not sure—"

"I can do it." The certainty coursed through my blood. Then I hesitated, glancing at Mom. "But, Mom, it's my fault you lost your job. It'll be my fault if we have to leave Marina Springs."

Mom shook her head. "It's no such thing. Mr. Sneeves has impossible standards. I don't need that kind of stress in my life, which is why . . ." She smiled shyly. "I have an interview at the Marina Springs Ice Cream Shop this afternoon."

"What?" I stared at her.

Her voice was laced with pride. "They're looking for a new ice cream manager and were impressed with my experience." She smiled. "And they've heard about our Fairy-Tale Ambrosia. Apparently it's trending on Snapchat?" She shrugged. "It has quite the reputation around town now."

I smiled. I'd have to tell Lanz. He'd be thrilled. A second

later, my smile waned, but then I brushed thoughts of Lanz aside. "That's great, Mom. I'm so proud of you."

"And I of you." She hugged me as the lunch bell rang.

"I better go."

She nodded. "Me too. I have to figure out what to wear to the interview." She smiled, looking sheepish. "And do you know what else I decided today? I'm going to start checking out some online dating websites."

"*Mom!*" I cried, feigning shock when really I was thrilled.

She laughed. "Don't worry. I'm not having a midlife crisis. I just want to get more of a life."

I hugged her. "Good for you, Mom. I'm *more* than okay with that." I pulled on my sneakers and tucked my pointe shoes into my schoolbag. As worn as they were, I'd have to make them last one more day. "So I'll see you at home after the rehearsal?"

She shook her head. "No. You'll see me *at* the rehearsal. I haven't seen you on pointe yet." She gave me one last hug. "I can't wait."

• • • • • • •

I unlocked the door to our apartment and rushed inside, adrenaline buzzing through me like a thousand happy bumblebees. If Signora Benucci said I could have the role back, would there be a Cinderella costume for me? What about my pointe shoes? And—biggest of all—what about Violet? Who was going to tell her about me dancing the part of Cinderella? Playing through every scenario of how she might react made my stomach liquefy. And through all my worry and excitement, Lanz was there, at the forefront of every thought.

Mom had given me my phone back, so I'd emailed him again today to tell him the latest news. But I hadn't gotten any emails back. His absence and silence were the only dark spots in my brightening mood. I wished I could talk to him face-to-face. I wished I could tell him exactly how I felt about him. I wished I could see his adorable curls again. I wished . . . I wished . . .

A demanding knock on the front door pulled me from my thoughts. I opened the door onto a perspiring, mottled Mr. Sneeves. He didn't bother with a hello, but instead blurted, "Is your mother here? I need her. Right away."

I stared at him. The nerve! As if he had any business asking after Mom, when twenty-four hours ago he'd fired her. "Sorry," I said curtly, "but she's at an interview right now. At the Marina Springs Ice Cream Shop."

"What?" He huffed. "Well. But. That's not—"

"You fired her. Remember?"

He dabbed at his forehead with a handkerchief. "But, but, I have an enormous ice cream order to fill at Once upon a Scoop!" His eyes turned pleading. "The Sanibel Resort wants fifty gallons of the Fairy-Tale Ambrosia for a wedding this weekend. The wedding is for the daughter of one of their best patrons. Everything has to be perfect. I haven't hired a new parlor manager yet, and no one else knows how to make the ambrosia!"

"That's a shame," I said flippantly. "It's the most popular item on the menu."

His face was streaming with sweat now. "I don't suppose . . . you don't know how to make it. Do you?"

I hesitated. I could tell him no, and let Once upon a Scoop bomb. But what about what the parlor meant to Mom? She'd given it so much of her time and energy. She was proud of the parlor and the way she ran it. And Lanz? The Fairy-Tale Ambrosia had been his invention. Maybe this was something I could do for him—a small gift I could give him in thanks. My heart made the decision for me.

"I'll make the ice cream," I finally said. "But only on one condition."

"Which is?" Mr. Sneeves asked impatiently.

"You tell my mom she can have her job back. She might not take it. She's heard great things about the salary and benefits at the Marina Springs Ice Cream Shop." Mr. Sneeves grimaced. "But . . . you promise to let her have it back. If she wants it."

Mr. Sneeves mumbled a string of indecipherables under his breath. "Fine. It's a deal."

"Good." I grabbed my rehearsal bag and phone, knowing that I'd need every second I had between now and six p.m. to churn that much ice cream. I'd have to leave straight from the parlor for rehearsal. As I swung the door shut behind me, I said, "Mr. Sneeves, I hope you like pineapple."

"Why is that?" he asked suspiciously.

I smiled. "Because you're going to be chopping a lot of it today."

· · · · · · ·

Three and a half hours later, I snapped the lid onto the last container of Fairy-Tale Ambrosia and set it in the subzero.

"That should do it." I turned to Mr. Sneeves, who was leaning against the counter, wiping his brow with his kerchief. As we'd been mixing the batches of ice cream, Once upon a Scoop had been swamped with an after-school rush of customers, and because I was the one who knew the Fairy-Tale Ambrosia recipe by heart, Mr. Sneeves was the one who had dealt with the customers.

Now he was kneading his hands, which were chafed and red from scooping. "I can't feel my fingertips," he mumbled.

"It's just a little frostbite," I deadpanned.

I nearly burst out laughing when he actually looked alarmed, but decided not to push my luck *that* much. "Kidding!" I said, then added, "soak them in some warm water for a few minutes and they'll feel better."

He raised an eyebrow at me, but didn't seem to have the energy for a rebuke. Instead, he surprised me by muttering, "Thank you. For making the ice cream."

I nodded. "You're welcome." I glanced at my watch. *Aue!* Rehearsal was in fifteen minutes, and it would *so* not be good to show up late, today of all days. "I have to go."

Mr. Sneeves stared at me in disbelief. "What? Now? But who's going to deal with customers until the parlor closes? And clean up afterward?"

I shrugged, stifling a smile. "What are *you* doing right now, Mr. Sneeves?"

I tossed him a pair of fairy godmother wings and a ruffly purple apron. Then, without another word, I left the parlor.

Chapter Sixteen

"Malie." Signora Benucci glided toward me. "It's so good to see you."

I smiled. "I'm so glad to be here." The studio was a bustle of activity; the entire *Cinderella* company was here and warming up to dance. I soaked in the soundtrack of the room—the chattering of the milling dancers, the classical music playing in the background, the muted thunking of ballet shoes on the wood floor. Omigod, I'd missed this place!

"First things first." Signora Benucci's tone was all business. "Do you feel you can do this? You've missed over a week of rehearsals. Normally I'd never allow this type of break in protocol . . ."

"I *know* I can." There was no room for doubt. Not if I was going to seize this chance.

She nodded. "We'll need Will for the *pas de deux*, and a run-through of Cinderella's dance with her mice friends. Now—"

"What's going on?" Violet was marching toward us, her expression indignant. If she still felt any worry over Mom losing her job, there was no sign of it now. "I just heard that Malie was getting her part back?"

"*If* she shows me that she can dance the part," Signora Benucci said.

"But I've had the part for over a week!" Violet cried. "You can't do this! It's so unfair."

"No," Signora Benucci replied matter-of-factly. "Unfair would be not giving her the chance to prove herself when she's missed rehearsals for circumstances beyond her control."

"But—but—" Violet held up a pair of silver glittering pointe shoes. "The costume's already been altered. And there's only one pair of Cinderella pointe shoes! There's no way Malie's feet are the same size as mine! Look!" She laid the shimmering silver pointe shoes beside my feet. It was obvious. They were much too small for my feet.

"I still have my pointe shoes," I said to Signora Benucci, "but the toe boxes are dead. I could wear them at the performance if I have to, but I'm not sure they'll hold up—"

"Will these do?" a voice said behind me.

My heart danced in my chest. No. It couldn't be—

I spun around to see Lanz standing there in the studio. He held a pair of glittering pointe shoes in his hand.

"I added a pair on to Mom's order form for you," he said casually, as if it was no big deal he was standing here, Stateside. As if he'd never been gone at all. "In case you changed your mind about dancing. I always had faith in you."

I couldn't wait through another word. "Lanz!" I threw my arms around him with so much force that we both staggered backward, nearly toppling.

"Wow!" Lanz laughed into my ear. "Now *that's* a welcome

home." He wrapped his arms around my waist. "What's this now? You didn't miss me, did you?"

"More than you know," I whispered into his ear. Heat rose to my face. "I didn't think you were coming back."

"*Ovviamente!* Of course! This is my home now. And I wasn't going to miss seeing you perform as Cinderella. Not for a million sundaes."

"But—but you left. You said you were going back to Italy to be with your dad—"

"For the week. For a visit. Mom picked me up from the airport a few hours ago." His eyes lit up in that familiar, disarming way, and it was all I could do to keep from throwing my arms around him again. "The annual gelato festival came to Milan this week. Dad flew me out for it." His smile widened. "We won an award for best new flavor. Fairy-Tale Ambrosia. Of course, Dad added a few new ingredients, marshmallow cream and—"

My second hug, tighter than before, muffled the rest of his words. Then I pulled back. Everything about him—his unkempt curls and velvet brown eyes, his cutely crooked teeth—seemed to have grown even more adorable in the time we'd been apart. Oh, my heart. It was a puddle.

"Did you get my email?" I asked softly.

A tenderness came into his eyes as he nodded. "You said everything I needed to hear." He tucked a finger under my chin, lifting it toward his face. I closed my eyes, and—

"Um, excuse me," Violet interrupted. "I hate to break up the reunion, but are we going to see whether Malie can dance this part or what?"

We stepped apart. My cheeks flamed as I realized Signora Benucci'd been witnessing everything with wide, wondering eyes. Now she cleared her throat delicately but meaningfully. "Yes. I see those English lessons have been going *very* well." She raised an eyebrow at Lanz.

"Now don't throw any shoes at me, Mammina," he laughed.

"Hmm . . . we'll talk later," she said, but she was smiling. "After this rehearsal, which we need to start. Now."

"*Va bene*," he said to her. "I'll go. But first . . ." He knelt at my feet. "*Adesso*, let's see if the shoe fits."

Gently, he unlaced my sneakers, and then slid on the Cinderella pointe shoes as I held my breath.

"Well?" He glanced up at me expectantly.

I flexed my feet, then slowly rose onto my toes in a *relevé*, testing the shoes. I smiled, feeling regal. "They're perfect."

"We'll see how you dance in them," Violet said stiffly.

Signora Benucci looked wary as she studied the new pointe shoes. "You haven't broken them in yet . . ."

"It's all right," I said. I flexed my feet again, knowing by feel that later, I'd have to crush the toe boxes. Instinct told me what I'd need to do to make them my own. "I can wear them for today." I looked at Signora Benucci. "I'm ready."

Violet gave an almost imperceptible huff as Signora Benucci nodded. "We'll start with the opening number."

Lanz offered me one last swoon-worthy smile before he left the studio. I smiled, my heart beating in anticipation of when I'd have my next moment alone with him. I wanted to hear about his time with his dad, and to fill him in on everything he'd missed while he was away. And—oh—I wanted that missed kiss.

But first, there was something I had to do. Instinct

sharpened my focus until that welcome, familiar feeling of intensity and purpose solidified my resolve.

Dance. This moment was for dance.

Signora Benucci readied the music while the other dancers moved to the outskirts of the floor to watch. I took my spot at the center of the room.

The music began, and, seamlessly, as if I hadn't missed a day's rehearsal, I danced. Everything that had happened in the last few weeks melted away, until it was my body and the music. Everyone fell into silence as they watched, but that didn't matter to me. Nothing mattered except the unbridled joy I felt.

I worked my way through the first three numbers before Signora Benucci called for a break. I glanced around the room and saw several people whispering, and Violet staring at the floor, looking uncharacteristically reserved. I held my breath, waiting, wondering if I'd done it.

"Malie." Signora Benucci smiled at me. "You are *our* Cinderella."

My heart thrilled, and I closed my eyes in gratitude, that I'd been given this second chance. "Thank you," I managed to whisper.

Then I caught a glimpse of Violet's lip trembling. I understood what that sort of disappointment felt like. I'd been where she was now, just one week ago.

I moved toward her, and before she could protest, I hugged her. "I'm sorry it can't be both of us." I meant it. "You're an incredible dancer."

"You are," Signora Benucci said to her kindly. "I'm hopeful that both of you may have futures in dance, if you keep working."

A stream of emotions crossed Violet's face—anger, frustration, disappointment—and I wondered how much of her demeanor was shaped by her fear of rejection. Maybe, underneath her stuffy exterior, she was simply fighting for her dreams the only way she knew how.

"You deserve the part," Violet said quietly, directing her words toward me without making eye contact. "*This* time. I knew it when I saw you audition. But—" She lifted her eyes to mine in a challenge. "Next season, expect some serious competition." She held out her hand.

I shook it. "We'll keep each other on our toes."

She snorted and rolled her eyes. "You should really leave the jokes to your boyfriend."

I blushed at the word, but I knew it fit Lanz perfectly. My heart belonged to him.

"All right, ladies," Signora Benucci said, her tone all business. "Malie, we need to get you fitted for your costumes. And now I want to run through all of your *pas de deux* combinations with Will. Violet, I want you dancing with your fairy godmother wings on. You need to get used to wearing them. Your balance will feel different with them on." When we didn't move quickly enough, she clapped her hands. "*Prontissimo*, ladies! We have much work to do."

I hurried toward the changing room, where I could already see the seamstress waiting with her measuring tape. Someone else was waiting for me, too. Mom.

"Malie," she breathed. "I—I'm speechless." She hugged me fiercely. "And so proud." She wiped at her eyes. "We'll buy you new pointe shoes first thing tomorrow! You'll have to save your Cinderella pointes for opening night."

"Mom . . . we can't—"

"We can." She grinned. "While I was at my job interview, I got ten voice mails from Mr. Sneeves. Ten! Begging me to come back to Once upon a Scoop."

I gaped. "No way. What did you say?"

"That I'd have to think about it." She sniffed. "Until he offered me twice the salary, two extra weeks' vacation each year, and agreed to let me hire three additional employees for the parlor."

My jaw dropped. "That's amazing!"

"Oh yes," she went on, "and you and Lanz can stay on, too. I'm giving Lanz the title of junior ice cream maker." She gave me a meaningful look. "But you won't need to work as many hours now, which means you'll have more time for this." She waved her hand at the studio. "As much time as you want."

My eyes welled with relief and happiness. After all this time, Mom finally understood me. Or maybe we finally understood each other better.

"Thank you." I hugged her again, my heart swelling. "I love you."

"I love you, too," she whispered. "I'll never discourage you from your dream again. That's a promise."

• • • • • • •

After the seamstress took my measurements for the costumes, I went back to the rehearsal. Mom stayed to watch some of it, then headed home to start dinner. The rehearsal was exhausting, but amazing. When we were done and everyone had changed back into their street clothes, I was the last dancer to leave the dressing room. I walked through the studio hallway, dance bag in hand, humming happily.

And then, standing before me, was Lanz. Right in the spot where we'd first met. I realized he was probably waiting for his mom, who was still in the office. Lanz and I faced each other, alone.

"Congratulations, Malie." He beamed at me, and I felt my heart jump again. "You did it! Your wish came true."

"You're right. Except . . ." I trailed off and blushed, not sure I had the courage to do what I was about to do. I felt as nervous as Cinderella before the ball.

"Except what?"

"I have another wish."

He whistled. "Now you're being greedy." I laughed, then he added, "If you need another wish granted, you better go find your fairy godmother."

I shook my head and my face blazed, but I pushed on. "Only *you* can grant me this wish." I stepped closer to him.

His eyes twinkled, but his face was serious. "What is this wish?"

"To have a kiss."

"From Prince Charming?"

I rolled my eyes. "This Cinderella doesn't need a prince to rescue her. But . . ." I smiled. "I'll take the kiss. From you."

"Now that," he whispered as he cupped my face in his hands, "is one *fantastico* wish."

He brought my lips to his, and the world spun. This was magic. Not fairy-tale magic, but a better kind—the kind that was real.

Epilogue

I stood in the wings, staring out at the stage. A dozen dancers in mouse costumes were taking their marks, getting ready for the curtain to rise. Behind them was a painted backdrop showing the castle, and an elaborately constructed fireplace prop. In just a few minutes, I'd be dancing by that fireplace, sweeping imaginary cinders from its glowing hearth.

"Hold still for one more second," Jen, the conservatory's seamstress, said around the needle and thread between her teeth. She was sewing me into the first of the five costumes I'd be wearing tonight—this one a long-skirted peasant dress that Cinderella wore before her transformation from servant to princess.

The backstage area buzzed with activity. Parent volunteers rushed from one dressing room to another, carrying heaps of tulle and sequined costumes while dancers added final sweeps of blush or lipstick to their stage makeup.

"Does anyone have more bobby pins?" Natalie, aka Cinderella's stepmother, called out as she fussed over a strand of hair that had sprung loose from her bun. One of the stepsisters came to her aid while the other panicked over a snag in her tights.

"One more pic," Violet said as she snapped a selfie with her friends, and then immediately set about posting it on social media.

Other dancers were stretching, or lacing up their pointe shoes. It was blissful chaos—the kind that made my blood sing with energy. I'd already gotten my good-luck hugs from Tilly, Andres, Mom, and Lanz. Andres had promised to film the entire ballet so that I could send it to Dad later, and so that Ethan and Eve could watch it when they got back from the Invention Convention. When the curtain rose, so many people I loved would be just beyond the spotlight in the front row, watching as I took my first steps as Cinderella.

Now, in these few minutes before the show began, I wanted to stand here, absorbing every detail and emotion of this moment. A few weeks ago, Cinderella had been my impossible dream, but now—at long last—the dream was happening.

"There," Jen said, and I felt a tug at my waist as she snapped off the last of her sewing threads. "All set."

I closed my eyes and took a deep breath, reaching into my core to bring up the strength and energy I'd need for the next two hours. Then I touched my hand to the delicate necklace Signora Benucci had allowed me to wear with my costumes— the necklace Lanz had given me. It felt like a good luck charm.

Signora Benucci stepped to my side then. "Are you nervous?" she asked.

"Excited," I said with a smile. "Beyond excited."

She smiled. "This is your moment, Malie. You've worked so very hard for it. Now. Savor it."

The opening music started, and Signora Benucci stepped into the shadows, blowing me a kiss with both her hands.

The curtain rose, and I *bourréed* onto the stage as the ballet began.

· · · · · · ·

It was like my dreams, only better. If my dreams were a stream of wishes, then this was an ocean—vast, powerful, and more beautiful than anything my imagination could conjure. I danced my way through the story of the cinder-girl transformed into a princess. I moved across the stage as the spotlight beamed down, dust motes glimmering gold around me like fairy lights.

I didn't feel the heat of the lights. I didn't feel the strain of the effort from my performance. My muscles, breath, heartbeat, bones—all of them were tuned to the swelling melodies. If it were possible, I would've wanted this performance to last forever. But all too soon, the final movement began.

My *pas de deux* partner, Will, raised me into a final lift, holding me so high that the spotlight felt like sun on my face. Below me, the rest of the company twirled on their toes, spinning in the grand finale.

My smile grew as Will slowly spun me to face the audience. I couldn't see Mom's gaze, but I could feel it—proud and full of love.

The music peaked in the final, rich note. I stretched my arms wider, extended my legs and back, making my body one long, graceful arc. I was a dancer, a dreamer. I *was* Cinderella.

The curtain slowly descended, and the audience exploded in applause. As soon as the red velvet brushed the floor, relieved laughter and hugs broke out among all us dancers. Will slowly lowered me to the floor and we congratulated each other and everyone around us. Then the company formed lines for our bows.

I waited at the back of the stage as the curtain rose again, and each line of dancers stepped forward to curtsy and bow. Finally, the rows parted in the middle to reveal me at the back. I walked to the front of the stage, then curtsied low to the audience.

The applause grew. I squinted down to see the front row, where Tilly was standing and cheering. Mom was there, too, her eyes shining with tears, and Andres was busy filming with his phone. And then there was Lanz, clapping wildly and beaming up at me. A warm joy filled me.

Signora Benucci came onstage then to take her bow, and we dancers applauded her, while Will handed her a huge bouquet of flowers. Then the curtain came down again, and we could hear the audience members rustling around as they stood up.

Some of the dancers lingered onstage, already chatting excitedly about the cast party. Family and friends from the audience flooded the stage, offering flowers and congratulations. Violet was in her element, accepting compliments for her role as the fairy godmother. I had already told my mom and Lanz that I'd meet all of them outside after I'd changed out of my costume.

As I headed into the wings, though, there was Lanz, waiting for me. He held out an enormous bouquet of pink roses that matched the color of my final costume—the glorious sequined pink tutu. I blushed and accepted the flowers.

"Thank you," I said, over the sound of my thundering heart.

He quickly kissed my cheek. "Your other gift is in the freezer backstage."

"Let me guess. Ice cream?"

"Of course not!" He winked. "Gelato. A brand-new recipe, named after you. Cinderella Stracciatella."

I laughed. "I love it already."

He grinned. "You were amazing. *Are* amazing."

A parade of mice dancers scurried by, de-whiskering and removing tails as they went.

"It looks like the fairy-tale spell is ending," Lanz said, watching them go.

"Not for me." I reached for his hand. "Thank you, Lanz. For everything. For telling me not to give up. For being the voice in my head that kept prodding me to stick with it."

"That voice was annoying, yes?"

"Very." We both laughed. "But also witty and likable."

"Irresistible?" He raised a hopeful eyebrow.

"I'll keep you posted."

He laughed again. "My sense of humor is rubbing off on you."

I shrugged. "I'm trying. But I can't compete."

"That is good. I can be the clown, and you can be the swan. Today, the Marina Springs Conservatory. Tomorrow, a professional ballet company."

"We'll see. I have a lot of things I want to accomplish. But I don't have to do it all today, or in a year, or even two years. For now, I'll take tonight."

He cocked his head at me. "That's enough?"

"More than enough." And I meant it with all my heart.

"One moment," Lanz said. He took my hand and led me down the hall toward the prop room, where there was a small fridge and freezer. Lanz opened the freezer and reached inside. "Your reward awaits." He held out the small pint of gelato and a spoon. "Ready to try?"

"Ready," I answered. Lanz scooped a curl of gelato onto the spoon, and I opened my mouth.

Yum. The gelato was rich and delicious, creamy and sweet. The perfect mix. Just like we were.

And the kiss that Lanz gave me next, as we stood backstage in our own *pas de deux*, was even sweeter.

ice cream
recipes

In the mood for a treat to melt your heart? Now you can create your own flavors at home! For all the recipes below, you will need a 4- to 6-quart home ice cream maker (can be found at any department store or online). Just remember to always have adult supervision when you're using a stove top or handling hot foods.

Here's the scoop:

Homemade Chocolate Ice Cream

You will need:

1 ice cream maker
4 eggs
2 $\frac{2}{3}$ cups granulated sugar
2 tbsps cornstarch
$\frac{1}{2}$ tsp salt
6 cups whole milk
1 heaping cup semisweet melted chocolate chips
1 $\frac{1}{3}$ cups half-and-half
2 cups heavy cream
2 tsps vanilla extract
Approximately 5 pounds of ice
Ice cream salt or rock salt

Before you start mixing ingredients, get your ice cream maker ready by removing the canister from the maker and chilling it in the freezer for 2 to 3 hours. Next, beat 4 eggs in a large mixing bowl. Then, in a large cooking pot, mix the sugar, cornstarch, and salt together. Slowly stir in the milk. Cook over medium heat just until tiny bubbles form around the edge of the pot. This is called "scalding." Stir constantly, being careful not to let the mixture come to a boil. Once tiny bubbles form in the milk mixture and it's steaming, carefully dip a measuring cup into the pot and fill it about 1 to 2 cups full with the hot liquid (an adult should help you with this step!). Very slowly pour the liquid from the measuring cup into the beaten eggs. If you pour too quickly, the eggs will overheat and curdle. Be patient. Only a trickle at a time! Stir the eggs constantly as you add the liquid. Next, slowly add the egg mixture back into the remaining hot liquid in the pot. Again, keep stirring so the eggs don't curdle! This can be a challenge on the first try, but don't give up! Now, continue cooking and stirring the liquid in the pot on medium-low heat for several minutes until the liquid steams and starts to thicken. Do not let it boil! While the liquid continues to heat, have a parent or helper melt the cup of chocolate chips in a microwave-safe container in the microwave. Microwave 15 to 20 seconds at a time, stirring in between, for about 2 minutes total. Stir chips until smooth and creamy.

Once your pot of thickened liquid is ready, remove it from the heat and stir in the melted chocolate. Whisk the chocolate and liquid together until it's smooth and blended. It should look a little like hot chocolate, but thicker! Next, add the half-and-half, heavy cream, and vanilla. Then cover and refrigerate for at least 2 hours (or even overnight).

Once the mixture is completely chilled, follow the instructions on your ice cream maker to make your ice cream. A parent's or caregiver's help may be needed to place your ice cream canister in your maker and get the ice cream maker plugged in and started. If you have a motorized ice cream maker, you will need to add ice and rock salt to the ice cream maker in order for it to work. There are different kinds of home ice cream makers, so be sure to read all of the instructions on yours thoroughly. Makes 4 quarts of chocolate ice cream.

Homemade Vanilla Ice Cream

You will need:

1 ice cream maker
2 cups whole milk
$1\frac{3}{4}$ cups granulated sugar
$\frac{1}{2}$ tsp salt
2 cups half-and-half
4 cups heavy cream
$1\frac{1}{2}$ tbsps vanilla extract
Approximately 5 pounds of ice
Ice cream salt or rock salt

Before you start mixing ingredients, get your ice cream maker ready by removing the canister from the maker and chilling it in the freezer for 2 to 3 hours. Next, in a large cooking pot, heat the milk over medium heat until tiny bubbles form around the edge of the pot. This is called "scalding." Stir constantly, and be careful not to let the milk come to a boil. Once tiny bubbles form in the milk and it's steaming, remove it from the heat. Mix in the sugar and the salt. Next, add the half-and-half, heavy cream, and vanilla. Then cover and refrigerate for at least 30 minutes (or even overnight).

Once the mixture is completely chilled, follow the instructions on your ice cream maker to make your ice cream. A parent's or caregiver's help may be needed to place your ice cream canister in your maker and get the ice cream maker plugged in and started. If you have a motorized ice cream maker, you will need to add ice and rock salt to the ice cream maker in order for it to work. There are different kinds of home ice cream makers, so be sure to read all of the instructions on yours thoroughly. Makes 4 quarts of vanilla ice cream.

For fun Once upon a Scoop ice cream flavors:

Once your basic chocolate and vanilla ice creams are made, you can separate the ice cream into smaller pint-sized or 1-quart quantities and add in any delicious ingredients you'd like to make some fun fairy-tale flavors. Be sure to mix in these ingredients when the ice cream is freshly churned and still soft. You can harden the mixed ice cream in the freezer afterward. Here are a few flavors you can try.

Fairy-Tale Ambrosia Ice Cream

1 to 2 pints vanilla ice cream
1 (8-oz) can crushed pineapple, drained
$\frac{1}{4}$ cup coconut macaroon cookies, chopped
1 (15-oz) can of tropical fruit salad
Unsweetened coconut milk (to taste)
$\frac{1}{4}$ to $\frac{1}{2}$ cup mini marshmallows (you can add in as many as you'd like)

Tiara-misu Ice Cream

1 to 2 pints vanilla ice cream
1 to 2 cups of store-bought or homemade tira-misu, cut into pieces
1 tsp coffee extract
1 to 2 tbsps Biscoff Cookie Butter (can be found in local grocery store in the peanut butter and jelly aisle)

Rumpeltwixkin Ice Cream

1 to 2 pints vanilla ice cream
$\frac{1}{4}$ to $\frac{1}{2}$ cup chopped Twix candy bars
$\frac{1}{4}$ cup Heath Bar bits
1 tbsp salted caramel ice cream topping

Goldichocs and the Butterfinger Bears

1 to 2 pints chocolate ice cream
$\frac{1}{4}$ to $\frac{1}{2}$ cup chopped Butterfingers
1 to 2 cups chopped Reese's Peanut Butter Cups
$\frac{1}{4}$ cup peanut butter chips

Turn the page for a sneak peek at Suzanne Nelson's novel *Donut Go Breaking My Heart*!

Sometimes friends, crushes, and film stars
aren't the sweetest mix . . .

donut go breaking my heart

suzanne nelson
author of *macarons at midnight*
and *hot cocoa hearts*

wish

SCHOLASTIC

Chapter One

Here it comes. The lightning strike of inspiration. The perfect idea. Wait . . . for . . . it.

I stared down at the rows of golden rings, breathing deeply. Their scent was like a sweet, doughy hug in the cramped but cozy kitchen.

Anticipation had kept me warm on the short, snowy walk here from my apartment on Sixth Street in Manhattan's East Village. I'd stayed up past midnight brainstorming without success, but I wasn't worried. One whiff of the fresh-baked goodness from Doughlicious was always enough to set my brain humming.

Helping out at the donut shop was a win-win; it meant I got to spend extra time with my BFF, Kiri Seng, whose parents owned Doughlicious. And my own parents approved. "Work will do her good," my dad had told my mom. "Talking to customers will force her out of her shell."

Well, the work might not have fixed my shyness, since I spent most of the time hiding in the kitchen instead of out front dealing with customers. But I got my best set-design ideas while I kneaded dough or drizzled icing. Last year, while baking donuts, I realized I could rig up a treadmill to create a moving yellow brick road for our school's production of *The Wizard of Oz*.

And now I needed another good idea. It would come. It *had* to come.

I lifted a still-warm donut from the tray and dipped it into a large bowl of caramel. Then I zigzagged melted bittersweet chocolate over the icing and added a sprinkling of sea salt for a finishing touch. I reached for the next donut, and the next after that. The rhythm of the motions had a hypnotic effect, and soon I was lost in thought, envisioning an empty stage, waiting for its perfect set.

A set design showing a fresh, distinctive take on Romeo and Juliet. That was what my application to New York University's summer drama program had asked for. My plan had been to work on the set model over winter break so that I'd be well on my way to finishing it before starting back at school. It was due by February 3. Three weeks from now. I wanted to get into this program *so* badly, more than anything else I'd wanted *ever*. That wanting seemed to be freezing up my brain, because so far, I hadn't come up with a single inspiring thought.

My hands kept moving, dipping in and out of the caramel bowl, but no lightning struck, no ideas came.

"Sheyda!" Mrs. Seng appeared at my elbow, smiling in approval at the now-finished tray of Caramel Dream donuts. "Perfect!"

I smiled back, reluctantly giving up on my quest for inspiration. "Thanks."

She winked. "You're my best icer. I tell Kiri all the time, 'Why can't you ice like Sheyda?' But she says actresses don't do donuts." I stifled a giggle as Mrs. Seng frowned. "My own daughter . . . hating the family business. What am I going to do with that girl?"

Find more reads you will love...

Although Ana doesn't have a dog of her own, she does get to walk her neighbor's adorable pug, Osito. One day, Osito befriends another dog at the park, who just happens to belong to a cute boy named Calvin. Ana implies Osito is hers, which seems like no big deal—until Calvin shows up at her school! Suddenly, Ana finds her fibs multiplying. Will she fess up before her white lies catch up to her?

TWICE UPON A TIME

Sleeping Beauty

*The One Who Took
the Really Long Nap*

WENDY MASS
Author of *11 Birthdays*
SCHOLASTIC

wish

Princess Rose has the worst luck. Though she avoided a fairy's curse for years, she ends up pricking her finger anyway and falling asleep for a hundred years. The Prince doesn't have it too easy either, especially with a mother who has some ogre blood. When he stumbles upon a certain hidden castle (and a certain slumbering princess), will it be happily ever after? Not until the Prince helps the Princess awaken . . . and brings her home to Mother.

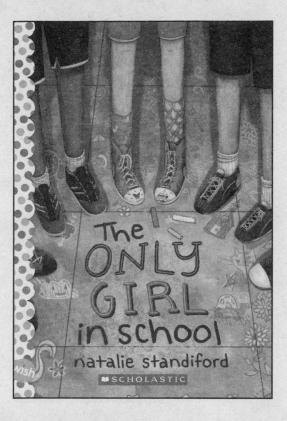

When Claire's best friend, Bess, moves away, she becomes the only girl in her entire school. At first, she thinks she has nothing to worry about. But then her other best friend, Henry, begins to ignore her, while a super-annoying bully and the boy who has a crush on her won't leave her alone. Claire is determined to show the boys that when it comes to thinking on your feet, she's got them outnumbered.